The
Hellhound Project

The
Hellhound Project

RON GOULART

DOUBLEDAY & COMPANY, INC.
GARDEN CITY, NEW YORK   1975

All of the characters in this book
are fictitious, and any resemblance
to actual persons, living or dead,
is purely coincidental.

Library of Congress Cataloging in Publication Data

Goulart, Ron, 1933–
The hellhound project.

I. Title.
PZ4.G692He   [PS3557.O85]   813'.5'4
ISBN 0-385-06275-3

DEDICATION: This one is for Sean.

There's a Hellhound on my trail.

The
Hellhound Project

CHAPTER 1

The mechanical cop came roving through the ninth floor of the Plaza Hotel, swinging his electric nightstick. "Time's up there," he said as he jabbed at the inhabitant of one plastic cot and then another.

Dawn light was beginning to show dimly at the barred windows of the large room. Heavy rain continued to fall.

A lean, scraggly man sat up, massaged his face with scabby hands. "I still got an hour, you dumb tin can." He pointed at the ticking meter beside his cot.

The robot flophouse cop rolled on, poking his stick into sleepers whose meter time had run out. "Time's up there. Rise and shine."

"Dumb bastard hardware." The scraggly man toppled back into sleep.

The mechanical cop was stopped beside another flopcot. "Rise and shine, up and at 'em. Off your ox, buddy." He repeated this twice before holstering his shock stick to grab at the fat man sprawled on the raveled thermal blanket.

From the next bed a black man in a tattered jumpsuit said, "You got yourself one for the Cadaver Service, cop."

"Time's up there," the mechanical cop told the fat man as he shook him by the shoulders. "Rise and shine, up and at 'em. Face the new day with a smile."

The black man, yawning and lowering his feet to the floor, said, "Cardiac thing, I'd guess."

Two cots to the left of the dead man, Thad McIntosh awoke. He shook his head from side to side, gulped in the thick, musky air of the flophouse. Thad was twenty-eight, long and lanky. Right now he was about fifteen pounds underweight, had a three-day beard, and a scabby scar on his forehead. He was dressed in a pair of thin track slacks and a surplus coat from the Brazilian war of 2018. Rubbing at his crusty eyes, he told the mechanical rouster, "The guy's dead; leave him alone."

The Negro grinned at Thad. "I'm glad you agree with my diagnosis of the stiff. Did you used to be a doctor?"

"Nope." Thad untied the laces of his all-season boots, which he had fastened round his neck for the night.

"I was. It's an interesting story how I fell from grace. I had—"

"It always is." Thad tugged his boots onto his bare feet, yawned.

"No, I didn't always live on Manhattan," continued the former doctor. "I had me considerable status one time."

"This man is deceased," announced the mechanical cop. His mouth clicking shut, he let the corpse fall back to the cot.

Thad ran a hand through his dark, tangled hair, wincing whenever he came to a lump or a bruised spot.

The lean, scraggly man was sitting up again. "Jesus, I don't like to be around when people die," he complained as Thad passed him.

"You came to the wrong island," said Thad.

"Who had a choice?"

The Plaza elevators still weren't working. Thad used the stairs. After three flights he found he was wheezing and panting. He halted on a landing, taking slow, careful breaths. Feeling absently into his jacket pocket he discovered a $20 silver piece. Enough for breakfast anyway. He had no recollection of why he had the money. It was his impression he'd stuck his last ten bucks into the bed meter. Smiling to himself, he continued on down.

The night doormen were going off duty, turning their stun rifles over to the three men on the morning shift. "Rained the whole frigging night," said the chunky doorman with red whiskers.

Campfires were smoldering all over Central Park, their smoke mingling with the gray rain and the thin light of this November daybreak.

"Maybe I should have slept in the park last night," Thad said to himself. "Then I'd have 30 this morning instead of 20."

A Cadaver Service doublegator ship came hovering down through the heavy rain to land at one of the entrances to the park. It retracted its wings, went wheeling through raw fields and bare trees to gather up the men who'd died there last night.

"On second thought," said Thad, "I guess I'm glad I didn't."

The faxprint robot who sold the Manhattan *Times* near the ruined fountain across from the Plaza was lying on its back, cashbox ripped open, alarm bell still faintly tinkling. Thad stopped long enough to make sure the looter hadn't missed any change, then moved on.

Another CS doublegator was flying low overhead. It

drifted on, landing on Fifth Avenue where there'd been a night-gang skirmish.

Farther along on Fifth a muddy cyborg hailed Thad. "Hey, Tommy, want to go in with us?"

Not slowing, Thad answered, "I'm not Tommy."

The man with the rusty metal arm squinted. "So you ain't. Well, what the hell, join us anyhow. We're loose and adaptable. We got us $42 toward a bottle of Sudafed. Alls we lack is another $33."

"Nope, sorry."

"Would you rather go in on a brain-stimulation jag? We could pool our dough for that and hit one of the bootleg brain-wave joints over in the UN building. Would you like that?"

"I'm trying to scrounge up breakfast. I'm broke."

Walking sideways beside Thad, the cyborg rubbed at the orange splotches of rust on his right arm. "A couple belts of Sudafed and you won't mind about chow. And if we can swing the brain thing, you'll come out thinking you had breakfast, lunch, and maybe a side order of soyfries."

Thad gave him a lazy salute, continued on his way faster. The rain kept on falling, cold and hard.

When he passed Alfie's Pub in the 50s, the battered old chef android out front said, "All you can eat, bo. Only fifteen smackers."

Thad slowed. The pub food wasn't that bad and $15 was a pretty fair price for breakfast, even though "all you can eat" probably meant a second slice of soy toast and an extra glass of nearjuice. Thad went inside.

The familiar smell of old wood and urine. One of the

stained-glass pub windows was still intact, and it threw watery kaleidoscope patterns on the bare noryl-plastic table tops. About a half-dozen run-down men were seated around the place. The scent of maple syrup was being piped out of the scent valves under the beamed ceiling.

Thad walked on back to the serving counter. A huge headless robot with six silver arms presided over the food. "Hot cakes, sausage, and hash browns," ordered Thad.

"Let's see the color of your money," said a voice from the speaker grid in the huge robot's stomach.

"Here." Thad held up his silver piece, gripping it right between thumb and forefinger.

A silver palm came extending out to Thad. "Put 'er there." A slot in the center of the hand glowed.

"Breakfast is only $15, isn't it? I get five bucks change."

"You'll get it. Fork over."

Thad stuck the money in the slot; the hand was withdrawn. He waited a few seconds before asking, "Where's my $5?"

"You ordered hot cakes, sausage, and hash browns," said the voice box. "You want those made out of soy or kelp?"

"I want my five bucks."

"Myself, I'd recommend soy."

"Damn it." Thad put his hands on the edge of the metal counter which separated him from the big servo-mechanism. "Give me my damn change and . . . ow!" An electric charge came sizzling through the counter. It made Thad fling his hands up, bite down hard with his teeth. He felt a little dizzy; his left leg didn't seem quite in control.

While he was still swaying in front of the big robot, two human hands grabbed his arms. "We don't like trouble-makers here, bud. Manhattan may be 99% crooks and deadbeats, but Alfie's Pub strives to maintain its tone."

"Give me my money."

"We're on to that dodge, too," said the large gray-haired man who had hold of him. "Out with you now, and don't come panhandling around Alfie's again."

"Goddamn it, you're not going to screw me out of the whole 20."

"Out, out." The big man hustled Thad to the door, shoved him into the rain-filled morning.

Thad went dancing backward across the rutted pave-ment, stumbled at the curb, fell on one knee into the gut-ter. He grimaced, rose up, his nostrils flaring. "That's my last 20."

A clean-shaven blond young man was standing in front of the pub entrance now. "Wait," he said.

"You another damn bouncer?"

"I have nothing whatsoever to do with this place," the blond young man assured him. "But perhaps I can help you." He put a hand against Thad's chest. "You're Thad McIntosh, aren't you?"

Thad blinked, then nodded. "Yeah. I don't know you, though. Do I?"

"I'm recruiting people for a—"

"Nope." Thad shook his head. "I don't want a job. I had one of those once, plus a wife and a house in Westchester County. That was back in . . . back in 2027, three long years ago. I don't want any of that anymore."

"This is only a part-time job," explained the young man. "A few hours work at most. We'll pay you $200."

"Two hundred dollars?" Thad took a step back on the wet street. "To do what?"

"A simple few hours work, work in your own line."

"I was an account man with Persuasion-Tronics. You're talking about some kind of ad work?"

"More or less." The blond young man slid a hand into an inner pocket of his waterproof tunic. "Here's $20. That was what you lost, wasn't it?"

Thad reached out for the silver piece. "Yeah."

"Think of this as a bonus for an anticipated job well done." From the same inner pocket he took a blue fax card. "You know where the library ruin is?"

"At 42nd and 5th? I've slept there quite a bit."

"There's a boarded-up soy-donut shop directly across. Take this card to Mr. Ferber there. He's doing our recruiting."

Thad pocketed the card. "How do you know I won't simply take your twenty bucks and wander off."

"I know enough about you to think you won't," replied the young man. "Besides, I can always find you again."

"How can you—?"

"Better get going. Mr. Ferber will be anxious to see you."

"Okay," said Thad. "Okay, and thanks." He started off in the rain toward 42nd Street.

CHAPTER 2

Rain was getting into the place. It dripped down through zigzag cracks in the low buff ceiling, sizzled around the dusty light-strip fixtures. The uneven thermal floor glistened with tiny pools of water. Shaking himself twice, Thad crossed the small room and stopped before the desk. There was no one behind the desk, but a dented old-fashioned secbox rested on the edge of the plyoblotter.

"Mr. Ferber, please," said Thad as he held out the blue fax card toward the machine.

"Wait your turn," replied the square black secbox.

There were four other men in the room, all older than Thad. There were three shaky-legged contour chairs. The fourth man sat on the wet floor, his legs forked straight out in front of him.

Thad told the machine, "I thought Ferber was anxious to—"

"Take a number and wait your turn."

Thad noticed a numbered chit easing out of a slot in the secbox's side. He took it.

The man on the floor mentioned, "You can get a cup of syncaf if you ask. While you wait."

Thad turned again toward the machine. "Can I get a cup of—"

A vinyl cup popped out of the back of the secbox and was filled from a chrome nozzle. "With our compliments."

The snycaf was lukewarm, though one of its additives caused it to give off steam. Thad carried it carefully over to a boarded-up window, then sipped at it. Through a slit in the nearwood planking he could see the one remaining stone lion on the library steps across the street. The lion's left ear was missing, and the rain was washing away the scarlet paint he'd been smeared with during the night. "What kind of job is this exactly?" Thad asked the man on the floor.

The man was forty-two, gray. He had two fresh gashes crossing his upper lip, and the teeth he was wearing weren't his. "Not exactly sure," he said. "Supposed to require some brains. Had some once. May still. Used to be a home-book-machine repairman in my . . ."

Thad squatted down beside the man and stopped listening. It was a knack he'd developed toward the end of his first year on Manhattan. He drank his tepid imitation coffee, let his eyes half close. After almost two hours his number was called.

Stretching up to his feet, Thad went into the next room. This one was a little larger, equally dusty and damp. A freckled man in a pinstripe tunic was sitting in an inflated sofa chair, a dictet unit resting on his knee. "Mr. Ferber?" Thad asked.

The freckled man glanced up. In a low voice he said, "Go on through that door on your right." As Thad went by him, the man asked, "How many more of those crumbums out there?"

Thad said, "I'm the last."

"Ah, great, splendid." The freckled man tossed the dictation machine to the floor. Rubbing the back of his neck, he said, "This kind of subterfuge always bores the . . . well, you better get on in there."

Thad walked through the indicated doorway into another dusty, rain-damaged room. A short, stocky man was pacing the bare floor, hands locked behind him. "How you feeling, McIntosh?"

"Hungry," answered Thad. "What kind of job is this going to be?"

"It's going to be a son of a bitch," the short dark man said. "I'm Crosby Rich."

"Oh, so?"

"You don't know me, but a lot of people, on and off Manhattan, do," said Rich, still pacing. "Which is why we had to play all these dumbbell games with you. Would you like a sandwich? I brought a half dozen with me."

"Sure." Thad watched Rich put a stubby hand into an imitation-wicker hamper on the floor. "You mean you're not interested in hiring any of those guys?"

"I'm not interested in hiring anybody. Except you, McIntosh," said Rich. "How about sealoaf on millet bread?"

"Anything's okay."

"When'd you eat last?"

"Lunch yesterday."

"Here." Rich tossed him the plyowrapped sandwich. "I've seen a lot of descents, McIntosh, but I really—"

"Talk about the job." Thad unwrapped the sandwich, took a bite. "Lectures I can always get."

The stocky man thrust his hand back in the hamper. "Huh, that was the last one. Did I down five sandwiches while I was waiting for you? Huh, going to have to watch that," he said. "I'm with the Opposition Party, McIntosh, working as a sort of troubleshooter."

Thad nodded, went on eating.

"We believe neither the Republican-Democrat Party or the Democrat-Republican Party can do much for the country. The RDs, since they've come into power, don't seem to be able to avoid a war with the South American Organization of States. We're headed right for it," Rich said. "You were a registered OP member."

"Back then," said Thad, chewing. "Before."

"So you probably agree with our positions on things. You no doubt share the goals which we—"

"Is this leading up to what you want to pay me $200 for?"

Rich sighed through nose and mouth. "Isn't your curiosity aroused at all, McIntosh? We go through all this dumbbell foolery in order to contact you quietly and covertly. Don't you wonder why?"

"Not particularly," Thad said, finishing the last bite of the sandwich. "You said you didn't have any more to eat? Tell you, Rich, after you've lived on Manhattan for a while you learn to exist in very small segments of time. To be curious much, you have to think of your life as extending some way in all directions."

"I still can't understand why you gave it all up," said Rich. "You were in a—"

"Got tired of it." Thad put his hands in his jacket pockets, leaned against the dust-smeared wall with one elbow. "What do you have in mind, Rich? You hoping to rehabilitate me?"

"Yes," admitted Rich.

"Put me back on my feet, exactly where I was before?"

The OP troubleshooter shook his dark head. "Not at all. I don't really give a rat's ass about that, McIntosh. Oh, I'm curious, but I didn't come here to do you a good turn. I'm here to see if you can do one for me. In order to do that you're going to have to stop being a deadbeat for a while."

"Only a while? Not permanently?"

"Once you do my job you can come back here and roll in any gutter you please."

"And it pays $200?"

"No, it pays $50,000," said Rich. "To start. And if you live through it, you'll get another $500,000 at least."

Thad straightened, rubbed both hands through his tangled hair. "A half million? That's not bad," he said. "But it sounds like this isn't going to take only the few hours your street man promised."

"It could take the rest of your life."

"You're implying the rest of my life may not be very long if I go to work for you?"

"Yes, there's that possibility. The plan we have in mind may not succeed."

Scratching his stubbled chin, Thad asked, "Okay, what is it you want me to do?"

"Basically," replied the stocky Rich, "you have to find out the nature of something called the Hellhound Project."

"Just how do I do that?" asked Thad.

"By being somebody else," Rich told him.

CHAPTER 3

The olive-green aircruiser flew clear of the rain and into bright afternoon sunlight. In the control seat Rich said, "I'm glad you agreed, McIntosh. It saves me from hunting down the other seven possibilities. You're the only one in the East. One fellow's out in what's left of Flint, Michigan, but we suspect the plague may have left him something of a dumbbell. The others are scattered all over the—"

"I haven't accepted the job." Thad was slouched in the passenger seat drinking a cup of syncaf. This one was hot. "I agreed to come over to Westchester with you to discuss the thing further. Long as you're going to pay me $500 merely for that, I'm agreeable."

"Look down on your left. We're flying over your old home . . . no, too late. Missed it."

Thad hadn't turned his head. "How come your cruiser says Olexo & Balungi, Para-Attorneys at Law on the side instead of Opposition Party?"

"Because if anybody found out what we're up to they'd probably kill me before I can do anything."

"Oh." Thad drank more of his imitation beverage. "Would they include me?"

"You especially."

"This Hellhound Project is so important?"

"Apparently," replied Rich. "We've lost five OP people this year. So far all we know is the name of the operation and the fact it's a new weapon of some sort being developed by one of the branches of Walbrook Enterprises."

"Took you five men to find out only that," said Thad. "I'm, all alone, going to uncover the whole story and come out alive?"

There were new lines on Rich's low dark forehead. "I don't guarantee you'll come out alive," he said. "Though if you ask me, you're not alive now, McIntosh. Huh, I've read up on you. An IQ of 185, a brain-potential score of . . . Okay, I promised no lectures." One stubby-fingered hand reached out to punch a landing pattern. "A fellow with your abilities, though, I still don't see why you—"

"I got tired." Thad slouched farther into his seat. "In fact, I have a feeling I may get tired of your job any minute now."

The olive-green cruiser drifted down through the clear sunshine, leveled, and went skimming over the tops of decorative all-weather imitation pines. "Westchester Country Club ⚡36," said Rich as the cruiser circled over the pink-paved landing area.

"They'll never let me in."

"The place is temporarily shut. OP is using it as a briefing depot until the government catches wise. Then we move again."

The cruiser bounced slightly twice, grew silent. The seat released Thad. Rising up, he asked, "What about food? Is there anybody around to fix lunch?"

Rich jumped free of the cruiser. "The servomechs are all in shipshape," he answered. "What's today, Tuesday?"

"I think so, why?"

"Tuesday is Mexican-American-style food. Each day is different; they're set that way. Do you like—?"

"My tastes have become catholic in the last couple years."

Two young men, casually holding stunguns, nodded at Rich from inside the main dome of the country club.

"Any trouble?" he asked, stepping inside.

"Nothing," one of them answered. "Dr. Rosenfeld called to say he'll be maybe an hour late."

"Huh." Rich led Thad up a twisting pastel ramp.

Thad asked, "Who's Dr. Rosenfeld?"

"Your family doctor."

"What family would that be? I never heard of the guy."

Rich stuck his thumb and little finger into a print lock on a corridor door. The door slid to one side. "I'll be briefing you in one of the dining rooms. You'll appreciate that."

"Don't get too feisty about my being hungry," suggested Thad as he followed the OP troubleshooter into a bubble-shaped room. "If I wasn't hungry, I wouldn't have come to you at all."

"Then we would have gone to you," Rich assured him. "Some subtle way or other." He marched to a long white table at the end of the room. It was the only rectangular table in a roomful of round ones. All the windows in the big room were set at black. "Sit down; we'll get started."

Thad took a tin chair two seats over from Rich and, without waiting to be told, dialed a meal on the order panel at his place. "Can I get you something?"

After a few seconds hesitation Rich said, "Not now,

thanks. Turn around so you can see those monitor screens
we've hung up on the wall over there."

Thad did. The second screen in a row of five showed
muddy-color footage of a young man, grinning, leaning
against the rail of some kind of seagoing craft. The young
man was lean, lanky, about the same size and build as
Thad.

"Look familiar?" asked Rich.

"Looks vaguely like me. Who is he?"

"Robert B. Walbrook."

"This must be old film. Robert Walbrook is fifty something. At least he was the last time I saw a newscast."

Rich flicked another toggle on the control rod he'd
picked up. The picture froze on a smiling closeup. "You're
looking at Robert Bruce Walbrook I," he explained. "This
film was shot fifty-one years ago, in 1979. That's Lake St.
Clair."

"Where?"

"It used to be near Detroit," said the OP man.

"Detroit I heard of," said Thad. "We lost Detroit . . .
when? . . . about six years ago, when that plague got
loose."

"Eight years ago."

"I've lost track." Thad gestured at the smiling image on
the screen. "So this Walbrook would be around eighty
today?"

"No," answered Rich, "he'd be in his late twenties."

"How does he work that?"

"Robert Walbrook was dying of leukemia in 1980. The
family, with Robert's consent, decided to try out a new

process Walbrook Enterprises had come up with. In fact, Robert was only their third subject."

"What did they do, freeze him? That was big back then."

"The Walbrooks' process was much more sophisticated," said Rich. "It involved placing the subject in a state of suspended animation, while he was still alive. Walbrook Enterprises thought of their process as something akin to cryptobiosis, a cryptobiosis which would work for human beings. Actually, the process worked quite well, but it cost so damn much it never caught on."

"Cryptobiosis. That's what some of the lower life forms can do to themselves, a kind of long-range hibernation."

"More or less. I didn't know you'd have heard of it."

"A guy with my potential?"

Rich continued, "So there was Robert B. Walbrook I, youngest of the three brothers who founded the whole Walbrook Enterprises operation. Lying in a suspension vault in a facility in one of the riot-secured sectors of Detroit. Actually the thing was in Grosse Pointe."

"When that experimental plague virus from the Flint proving ground got loose, it pretty much finished off Detroit and environs." Thad's Mexican-American meal had just popped up through the slot in the banquet table. Picking up the noryl-plastic utensils, he commenced eating.

"That's why OP is going to try what we're going to try," said Rich. "Something over two and a half million people died; there was three solid weeks of rioting, looting, and indiscriminate smashing carried on by the people the plague didn't kill right off."

Swallowing, Thad asked, "The vaults where Robert was stashed, they got destroyed?"

"Right down to the ground. The two-dozen bodies stored there were never accounted for."

"So nobody knows what happened to Robert I?"

"Nobody we've been able to check, nobody in the Walbrook family certainly."

Thad set his fork down, leaned back from the table. "And four years ago we finally got a cure for leukemia."

"Five years ago actually, but you get the point. If Robert Walbrook I's body had survived, they'd be able to revive and cure him."

"Would they really want to, the family?"

"Not all of them, but the way the resurrection laws stand at the moment, they'd have to," replied Rich. "Some of the younger members of the clan might be opposed. Especially a lad named Lon Walbrook, a grandnephew of Robert I, who's making a bid for more power. See, if Robert I shows up he's still technically one of the heads of the whole operation."

Thad rubbed at his shaggy hair. "So you Opposition Party guys are going to try to convince the whole family, the entire rich, powerful Walbrook clan in their fortified 200-acre estate in Connecticut, that I'm their long-lost boy?" He laughed, locking both his hands on top of his head. "Some kind of Tichborne claimant come back from the dead. Shit. It'll never work. They'd know I'm not—"

"Sure, looking at you the way you are now. A brokedown dumbbell from Manhattan. The smell of you alone would ruin it."

Still laughing, Thad went back to eating. "When I

finish here, you can give me my 500 bucks and a lift back
to my run-down contemporaries."

Rich moved to the chair next to Thad. "We'll work on
you before you ever have to meet the Walbrooks,
McIntosh," he said. "The physical work alone will take
two three weeks; the operations."

"Operations?"

"Facial work, fingerprints," Rich explained. "We'll have
to plant some pretty near foolproof caps on your eyes to
fake the retinal patterns. Brain-wave patterns we can't do
anything about. We're not certain anybody ever got Robert I's down and filed away. Then there's the—"

"How did you come to pick me?"

"Our computers did that, using info siphoned from the
national data bank. As I told you, you're one of a half-
dozen or so possibilities. Fellows who come near to Robert I in build, facial structure."

Thad wiped his plate clean with a fold of nearcorn tor-
tilla. "Can I order some more food?"

"Go ahead." Rich looked away. "The thing is,
McIntosh, we have every reason to believe the Hellhound
thing is a pretty nasty weapon. Warren Parkinson has
three more years to serve."

"Who?" Thad was ordering another meal.

"Parkinson, the President of the United States," said
Rich. "You know he's had two severe breakdowns since he
took office. He may even be in worse shape than anyone
suspects. We can't let something like the Hellhound
weapon fall into the hands of a man as unstable as Warren Parkinson."

"Maybe, despite its name, the Hellhound Project is something harmless," said Thad. "Walbrook Enterprises turns out a lot of stuff."

"This is a weapon, and it isn't harmless."

Thad's second meal appeared before him out of the slot. "How long would it take to turn me into a reasonable facsimile?"

"Six weeks at least, that's the minimum. A lot of background info can be put in while you're asleep."

"You'll provide me a comfortable place to sleep," asked Thad, "plenty of food?"

"Sure, and we'll rehabilitate you."

"That's unlikely," said Thad. "Still, winter's not so far off. This would take care of most of my winter problems."

Rich said, "Maybe you're tired of the life over there, McIntosh. Maybe you feel—"

"No lectures, no sermons." After eating for a moment, Thad asked, "Suppose I turn you down? Aren't you afraid I might talk to someone?"

"Should you not accept this OP job," Rich informed him, "you won't remember any of today. We have a process for that."

"I figured as much," said Thad. "Suppose the Walbrooks don't accept me; suppose they see through our great impersonation? Do I still get paid?"

"If you survive, yes."

"How do we explain where Robert . . . where I've been these years since the plague hit Detroit?"

"We have a relatively plausible story worked out. You'll be briefed on it, quite sufficiently briefed."

Giving a one-shoulder shrug, Thad said, "Okay, I'll try it. Doesn't make much difference I guess, not to me anyway. Sure, okay. When do we start?"

"Now," said Rich.

CHAPTER 4

"You're a fake!" accused the loud froggy voice. "You're not Robert Walbrook!"

Thad turned, grinned as much as his facial bandages allowed. "What kind of good morning is that, Dr. Leader? I'm just—"

"I said you're not Robert Walbrook! You're an impostor." The thickset, frizzle-haired doctor came lumbering toward him. The zigzag light strips on the ceiling made him glow faintly blue. "You damn well better come up with a good explanation of just exactly who you are!"

"Come back after lunch if you want to play games," Thad told him. "This second tinkering job they did on my face hurts somewhat more than you and Crosby Rich prom—"

"You'd be dead now!" shouted the doctor. "Dead and flat on your ass on the floor there if I'd been one of the Walbrooks."

"I'm not expecting any of them down here in our hideaway." He nodded at the windowless metal walls.

"That doesn't sound like Robert Walbrook. That's gutter flippancy."

"Bullshit. That's at least middle-class flippancy, Leader."

Dr. Leader stood over Thad's lucite rocker. "You're not Thad McIntosh anymore. Your life, which I don't care all that much about, and the success of this operation depend on your staging of the character of Robert Walbrook. Perhaps I ought to show you the expense printouts on this little venture."

"I don't care what it costs."

"Ah, that's more like it. That's Bobby Walbrook talking." The doctor reached out to run dry stubby fingers across Thad's face.

"Ouch."

"Coming along very well," the doctor said. "But that's not my department. I've got to drill you in impression management."

"Play-acting."

"Yes, that's right. You're putting on an act," said Leader. "You have to be perfect, and you can never let down and relax." From out his tunic pocket he suddenly grabbed a parasite-electric razor. Tossing it to Thad, he said, "This thing won't work. Beats me why."

"The chip's been removed."

"Good, very good. Robert Walbrook would know that, since this type of razor was in use when he was put to sleep."

Thad tossed it back to him. "You've got a shaggy patch under your chin. Might use this thing on it."

"You're getting the right touch of insolence into your voice," said Dr. Leader approvingly. "I saw your brother Gil this morning and he asked me to—"

"Gil's been dead for two years. If you saw him he couldn't have—"

"You don't know that! You have to wait until they tell you that. As far as you know, he's alive and kicking." With his tongue pressed against his teeth the doctor whistled a few bars of a tune. "Recognize that?"

"Nope, can't say I do."

"That's funny; it was very popular eight or nine years ago."

"We didn't have much music in the tomb, Doc."

"Yes, adequate response." Leader nodded his flamboyantly haired head. "Who's this?" He'd yanked a hand-briefer out of another tunic pocket and was projecting a color picture of a naked seventeen-year-old girl on the wall of Thad's room.

"Do I have to tell you? We hushed the business all up. In fact, I don't see how you even got hold of that photo of Molli," said Thad. "You've got the picture reversed, by the way. The freckle was under the left nipple and not the right."

"Excellent, excellent. The sleepbriefings are starting to produce results."

"Beg pardon? We were chatting about Molli. I don't quite understand this other stuff about sleep—"

"Very good." Dr. Leader walked away from him. Spinning around, he said, "You don't have to keep this up with me, Thad. We're friends, after all, aren't we?"

"Name is Robert. And you're no friend of mine."

The doctor laughed a froggy laugh. "Remember that it's dangerous to become sympathetic with your audience." He came back toward Thad. "Everyone you encounter in that Walbrook house—everyone—is part of your audience. There must be a distance between you, an invisible row of footlights. You're putting on a show, and you are never to cross that line. Once you start thinking of any member of your audience as a person, you're going to disrupt your performance."

"I'm aware of that," said Thad. "If my performance gets disrupted, it's me who's going to get knocked off. You can shrug and go back to . . . where is it you teach?"

"You don't need to know that," Leader told him. "Once I finish with you, whether you succeed or not, we'll never meet again. Who's that?"

He flashed a new picture on the wall. It was a slim dark girl of about twenty-four, fully clothed.

"Looks like she might be a Walbrook, but I don't know her." Thad dropped to his own voice. "Actually it's Jean-Anne Walbrook. I'm not supposed to know her, since she was born long after I was put on ice."

"You have to work on your unconscious gestures, Thad," warned Leader. "Watching you when I threw the picture at you, I was aware that you recognized the girl. You've got to work on that. Nobody must tumble to the fact you've been briefed on the entire Walbrook family."

"Okay," said Thad. "She's pretty, isn't she?"

Leader clicked the picture off. "She's part of the audience," Leader reminded him. "The audience is neither attractive nor unattractive. The audience is something to be manipulated and managed."

"Okay, so she isn't pretty," said Thad.

Thad thrust his bandaged hands, gingerly, into the pockets of his red neowool mackinaw. Light snow was starting to fall down across the morning. He stood still for a moment in the slanting forest of maples, then headed back downhill toward the big red barn. A few small year-round brown birds hopped out of his way.

A landvan came rumbling into view around a corner of the barn. It was battered, a peeling green. Nostalgia-on-Wheels was lettered on its side, along with Connecticut's Best Antique-Mobile. The van chuffed to a halt a few feet from the barn's open doorway. Crosby Rich climbed out.

"Up here," called Thad from the edge of the wood.

The Opposition Party troubleshooter shielded his eyes with a mittened hand, watching Thad approach.

Snow continued to drift slowly straight down.

Tugging off a mitten with his teeth, Rich reached the bare hand into his overtunic. "I got a half-dozen maple donuts at a stand down on Route 7. Want one?"

"Nope." Thad stopped a few feet in front of the stocky man. "They've got me back on a regular eating schedule here."

After taking a large bite out of the fat maple donut he'd produced from his pocket, Rich said, "I guess I eat from different motives than you, McIntosh." He stepped nearer to him. "You look terrific . . . I mean for our purposes. You're nearly an exact replica of that Walbrook dumb-bell."

"Does that mean we can cancel a few of the upcoming facial-surgery sessions?"

Nodding affirmatively, Rich said, "So they tell me. I'd say probably only one more, or two at the most. You've also made the weight, huh?"

"Yeah, I've gained eleven and a half pounds since I've been here," replied Thad. "Which makes me the exact weight Robert B. Walbrook I was when they laid him to rest."

Rich paced out a straight line on the snowy ground. Turning, he rested a shoulder against the dented side of his antique-mobile while he finished his donut. "The traditional time for reunions," he said, "is the Christmas season."

"Only three weeks off. You aiming to have me descend on the family by Christmas?"

Cocking his head at the red barn, Rich said, "They tell me you're making terrific progress. In a way, McIntosh, that still astounds me somewhat. I figured you for merely another Manhattan deadbeat, but you're showing—"

"If I'm going to do this job, I might as well do it right," Thad told him. "If this impersonation doesn't work, it's me they're going to knock off. So it's to my benefit to come across convincing."

Rich reached again into his pocket. "Sure you don't want a maple donut? This is the last one."

From the doorway of the slightly lopsided old barn someone coughed. A middle-sized, middle-aged man, wearing a mackinaw similar to Thad's, said, "Good morning, Mr. Rich. It's time for another of Mr. McIntosh's wide-awake briefing sessions. If that meets with your—"

"Sure," answered the OP troubleshooter. "I'll sit in."

They went into the barn and down through the opening in the floor.

"Accident prone," remarked Thad.

The OP briefer clicked off the view wall in the tin-walled underground room. "You did very well on the

Walbrook family tree this morning, Mr. McIntosh. No slips, nary a hesitation."

Wiping his slightly sticky fingers on the underside of his aluminum rocker, Rich said, "There have been a good number of accidental deaths in the clan over the past decade, haven't there?"

"Down to, and including, old Gilbert Walbrook himself two years back," Thad said. "Gil and I and Johnny started Walbrook Enterprises together, the three brothers. It's too bad he didn't live to see my return."

Rich frowned in the direction of the briefer. "Dig up some more background on these . . . how many was it?"

"Seven," said Thad, "if you include Cousin Miriam."

"Seven accidents in the Walbrook family since around 2018 or so," Rich said.

"You feel such information will aid Mr. McIntosh in better carrying on his role?"

Thad said, "Might also keep me from having an accident myself."

A tin door slid open to admit a thickset man of thirty-five. He, too, was wearing a neowool mackinaw, plus a red neowool cap with floppy earflaps. Under his arm he carried a twine-tied bundle of microcards. "You know what you've got in that antique van of yours, Crosby?"

"You been diddling around in there, Caruso? A bell's supposed to ding if anybody diddles around."

Caruso chuckled as he dropped the bundle of cards down on the copper table which held the microreader. "If I can't outwit a little simple-minded dingbell, Crosby, I'll retire," he said. "But you know what you—?"

"Those antiques are props for my cover story," said the

Opposition Party troubleshooter. "I travel through Connecticut so much because I'm a roving—"

"An authentic Kenmore 2-speed, 3-cycle washer is what you've got," said Caruso. "It has to date, based on a very quick appraisal, from 1970 to thereabouts. Even though Sears made thousands of those, they're awfully tough, to—"

"You can't take any of my props, Caruso."

"I collect the damn things, Cros. Listen, I'll give you $10,000 for it," persisted Caruso, "$10,000 for the OP campaign fund."

"That's a dumbbell thing to do. No old broke-down, last-century washing machine is worth even that much."

"You don't realize how much it would cost to buy an authentic Kenmore from a—"

The briefer coughed. "Perhaps you'd like to present your part of this morning's series of tests and explanations, Mr. Caruso."

"I'll talk to you again before you take off," Caruso told Rich. "Now then, Thad, I've been able to round up some more floor plans and design drawings of the Walbrook estate buildings. Including, fortunately for us, the layout of one of the rooms where they store information." He inserted a card into the reader.

Thad came over to look.

"I could maybe go as high as $15,000," Caruso said toward Rich.

CHAPTER 5

Dr. Barney Rosenfeld took his hands off the controls of the landcar and locked them on the top of his grizzled head. "You're you're on your own from here on, friend," he said, in his characteristic speech style. "The sound sound pickups will be trained on us once we get through the the gates." He was a moderately overweight man of thirty-six, his sand-colored hair speckled with gray.

Thad nodded, not saying anything. Directly ahead of them rose stone walls, made of the same large black and gray rocks you still saw throughout this part of Connecticut. Only these walls were higher, rising ten feet at least. Heavy gates, made of real wrought iron, barred their entry to the Walbrook estate. Just beyond the gates Thad could sense a force screen in operation. The light snow which was flickering down through the afternoon melted away to nothing when it came near the gates.

"I've got an identification plate implanted in the the hood of the car," explained the doctor. "They they're reading it now."

"They?"

Rosenfeld tilted his head in the direction of the wall. "The security robots."

A low ratcheting sound commenced outside; the metal

gates swung slowly inward. The landcar jerked, swaying slightly to the left before it starting moving ahead.

"They they've taken over the operation of the car now," explained the Walbrook family doctor.

The landcar proceeded slowly along the black roadway. The force screen was no longer there. When they had traveled some five hundred feet the car abruptly stopped.

"Stick stick one of your hands out the window, friend," advised Rosenfeld.

The car windows automatically rolled themselves down. Standing on each side of the vehicle now were robots. Each of them was man-size and dun-colored.

"Hand please," requested the one on Thad's side. He had a fine dusting of snow on his cheeks, shoulders, and chest. His metal hand was ice cold.

A small cone extended itself, with a raspy click, out of the robot's palm. A tiny blue light at the cone's end scanned the tips of Thad's fingers. The robot let go, saying, "Agrees."

Thad allowed himself to exhale.

A second later Dr. Rosenfeld's robot said, "Agrees."

The car windows shut; the machine rolled forward.

"That that was to check our finger fingerprints, friend," said the doctor.

"I figured."

Dr. Rosenfeld placed his hands back atop his head. "They they like to be able to see your hands."

Thad was scratching at his crotch with his counterfeit fingertips. "I think I'm going to have to make a few changes around the old homestead," he said. "A half century hasn't made Johnny any less of a fussbudget." That last word was one which had been current fifty years before.

"You you can't talk—" Dr. Rosenfeld stopped, remembering who Thad was supposed to be. "Yes, friend, you can certainly talk to JP about that. Although, as I've told you, the world hasn't improved measurably since you were alive last. There's even more need for security to-day."

"I suppose Johnny is up to his ass in government work still."

"I I believe so, yes," answered Rosenfeld, watching Thad through slightly narrowed eyes. "Though I'm only one of several several family doctors and I'm not in on any Walbrook secrets."

After their landcar climbed two low hills, the buildings became visible. A complex of six enormous white salt-box-type houses, connected by see-through tunnels. Stretching away behind the houses were acres of real trees—maples and birches—all bare and thin in the cold light.

"Johnny's expanded a lot I see," said Thad. "In my day we made do with only one house, the farthest one on the left there, and about thirty acres."

"Fifty years of nothing nothing but success can—"

"What are those new salt boxes made of?"

"Walbrook nearwood, I imagine."

"Since my time," said Thad. "I've got a lot of new products to get myself filled in on."

Their car was jerked off the roadway into a wide, circular clearing beside the big square house Thad was pretending to remember.

Two more robots, chrome-plated this time, helped them

out of the landcar. "House 1," said the robot who took Thad's arm.

Thad pulled free, went jogging off toward the connecting tunnel between the first and second houses.

"House 1," the robot called after him.

"Can that be little Muffin?" Thad was laughing.

Inside the nearglass tube-tunnel a thin, dry woman of fifty-six was setting out real plants on a series of hanging shelves. She glanced up, eyes going wide, and dropped an ivy plant. Pressing her palms against her narrow chest, she said, "My God, it's Uncle Bobby!"

Thad couldn't hear the words, but he could tell what she was mouthing. "It's me sure enough," he shouted back. "And you must be Muffin, all grown up. But still with that golden hair."

Cornelia Walbrook touched at her short-cut hair.

The chrome robot caught up with Thad. "House 1," he said once again.

"I'll see you inside soon, Muffin." Thad allowed himself to be guided back to the door of the first house. "As I recall I was working on a way to instill some sentiment into servomechanisms when I went away. I guess Johnny didn't follow that up."

"We should be taken to see your your brother now," said Dr. Rosenfeld.

In the foyer of the big white house a large blond man stood. "You're the alleged Walbrook, huh?"

"You're not kin." Thad turned to the doctor. "I thought Johnny was ready to see me."

"This," said Rosenfeld, "is is Mr. Gunder, with the United States Government."

"Agent Lyle Gunder," the large man amplified, "with the Total Security Agency. I serve as a liaison between Walbrook Enterprises and the government. I screen people." He strode up to Thad. "Before you go any farther I'm going to run a few tests on you."

"What what's this all about?" demanded the doctor. "I conducted—"

"The old guy himself ordered it." Gunder jerked his head at Thad. "You'll have to come along to House 2. By the way, what was your favorite vegetable as a kid?"

"Crooked-neck squash." Thad began to roam around the white room. "All the pictures have been moved."

"What was the name of your favorite stuffed toy when you were three?" asked the big TSA agent.

"Doggie."

"You had a crush in the second grade. What was her name?"

Shaking his head, Thad grinned. "You tell me. I never could remember girls' names. Even some of the ones I married and almost married are very dim."

"Which knee did you—"

"Don't let them wear you down, unc." A tall, smiling young man came in through a side door. He was about Thad's age and looked something like Thad, the altered, worked-over Thad. But he was thicker and there was a difference about the upper part of his face. "I believe in you. Purely on faith, since I wasn't even born until long after they stuck you on ice."

"It wasn't ice," corrected Dr. Rosenfeld. "Actually—"

"I know, Doc," said the young man. "I'm Lon Walbrook, unc." He clutched Thad around the shoulders. "Bob II's boy. You remember my dad, don't you?"

"A shadowy little boy," said Thad. "He used to like to suck the tips of felt markers."

"That sounds like Pop, unc. Except he's less shadowy now," Lon said. "He's really developed balls in the past few years. He's down in South Amer—"

"Stop hugging this alleged great-uncle of yours," said Gunder. "I've got to get him over into the research rooms right now."

"Is this any way to treat the walking dead, Gunny?" Lon stood aside while Gunder led Thad away toward another door. "I'll see you again up in JP's lair later, unc. I'm afraid you'll find poor Gramps hasn't held up as well as you."

"I've had a lot more rest."

Lon laughed. "I can see I inherited my sense of humor from you, unc."

"What was your best subject in junior high?" asked the large Gunder. He opened the door and stepped through.

"Paddle tennis." He followed the TSA man down an orange-tinted plastic tubeway.

Dr. Rosenfeld brought up the rear, saying, "I'm I'm still darned if I can see why you have to . . ."

Gunder grabbed open the door at the passway's end. "Why the hell are you here?"

When Thad stepped into the domed anteroom of House 2, he saw a lanky light-haired man smiling tentatively at him from far across the room.

The man held a bulky plyocovered folder tight against

his chest. "Hello," he said across the hollow distance. "Hello, I'm . . . uh . . . well, hello, Father."

Thad grinned, walking toward the tentative man. "You must be my boy, my son Alex." He reached out a hand to the fifty-five-year-old Alex Walbrook.

"Yes . . . uh . . . that's who I am, Father." He shifted the folder up toward his armpit. He lost control and it dropped, flapping, scattering microcards. "Sorry . . . uh . . . this is all rather awkward, isn't it? Encountering my own father again after so long . . . and . . . uh . . . here you are younger than I am." He started to bend toward the fallen materials.

Thad caught his hand and shook it. "It's good to see you, Alex. You've turned out well."

"Oh . . . uh . . . I really don't know, Father," said the son of Robert I. "If you'd been around . . . uh . . . I think I might—"

"Get that crap gathered up," suggested Gunder. "What are you moping around down here for anyhow?"

On his knees, Alex replied, "Well, Lyle, I was . . . uh . . . I was in the file—"

"There's an extensive amount of information filed here in House 2," said Dr. Rosenfeld to Thad. "Several several file rooms down that blue corri—"

"Enough chitchat," said Gunder. "I want to get this guy in where we can check him out real good. Fingerprints, eye patterns, the works."

Alex rose lopsidedly up, leaving most of the tiny file cards on the plastic mosaic floor. "Well, I'm . . . uh . . . happy that you're back, Father."

"So am I." Thad patted the lanky man on the shoulder.

"Save your hugging and kissing until we figure out who this guy is for sure."

"You . . . uh . . . ought to remember, Gunder, that I'm . . . uh . . . part of the Walbrook family."

"Uh . . . oh . . . uh . . . really?" laughed the TSA agent.

Thad took hold of Gunder's arm, pressed. "Let's take our tests."

"I feel this is redundant," said Dr. Rosenfeld, trailing the two of them to the wide yellow door of the test rooms.

During the next hour, six machines, two robots, three human lab technicians, and a Negro-tinted android examined Thad. After that, Gunder asked him to wait in an alcove room off the enormous gray-metal test lab.

"This is quite a setup," remarked Thad as Gunder slid the accordion door shut. "Built it just to run me through?"

"We can do a lot of things down here." The blue door closed tight.

Thad slouched in a rubber chair, watching the gray unadorned ceiling. He rubbed at his naked backside.

About ten minutes later Gunder returned. "Come on out here, buddy."

Thad strolled barefooted back into the larger room, followed Gunder around assorted mechanisms.

"Show this thing your hands again." Gunder jerked a thumb at the large tank-shaped machine which had tested Thad's fingerprints and palm patterns earlier.

Swallowing, Thad eased both hands into the waist-high slots. He hoped the Opposition Party technicians had done as good a job as Crosby Rich claimed.

The tank whirred, hummed, then made a faint whistling sound out of someplace around back.

"Well?" demanded Gunder.

"Perfect match," announced the speaker grid of the machine. "This man and Robert Walbrook I have identical prints."

With lips pressed tight together, Gunder took a deep breath. "Then why did you want to check him out again?"

"Well, actually he has a fascinating life line. I predict he's going—"

"Oh, shit." Gunder jerked Thad's hands free of the machine.

"Do I pass?" grinned Thad.

Gunder turned his back, gathered up Thad's clothes from a nearby chair top. "So far, buddy, so far, but I got a lot more tests in mind for you." He threw the clothes at Thad. "Some you won't even be aware of."

"Sock," said Thad.

"What?"

"You left one of my socks on the chair there."

Gunder snorted, went striding away.

CHAPTER 6

Thad and Dr. Rosenfeld, accompanied by Lon, moved through nearglass tunnels and salt-box houses, reaching finally House 6.

A chubby pink man with an aluminum right arm was awaiting them at the second-floor landing, shuffling almost imperceptively on the thick, flowered carpeting. "I am Badjett, sir," he said to Thad.

Lon asked, "Badj, aren't you going to hug the prodigal?"

"I am only in my very early fifties, sir," replied Badjett. "Therefore I never had the pleasure of serving Mr. Robert I. Come this way, if you will." He motioned to Thad with his metal hand.

Lon followed. "We're all going to call on Gramps."

Badjett raised his left eyebrow. He stopped in front of a real oak door, inserted a metal finger in the keyhole. The door swung inward.

The first person Thad saw was not old John Phillips Walbrook but a slim young girl. She was standing beside a high window, a dark girl with long black hair. The glare of the declining sun on the snow outside made a blue glare all around her. When she turned to face Thad he couldn't see her clearly, yet he knew there was something special about her. The way she held herself, the way she moved toward him.

"Uncle Robert," she said in her gentle voice. "We're all so very glad you've returned to us." She was about twenty-four and very pretty, in a quiet, delicate way. Much lovelier than she'd looked in briefing-session pictures and film clips.

"Company manners today, sis?" laughed Lon. "This is my sister JeanAnne, unc. What are you calling yourself of late, sis? Have you gone back to Walbrook?" He patted Thad on the shoulder. "You're in luck today. I stayed home from Walbrook Enterprises to greet you, and sis is here between marriages. It's too bad Dad couldn't get back from South America in time to—"

"Won't you come this way, Uncle Robert," invited the lovely dark girl. "Grandfather is very anxious to see you."

"This is her lady act, unc," said Lon. "Fools all and sundry until they—"

Thad took hold of Lon's arm just above the elbow and squeezed. "I suggest you adopt a respectful silence in the presence of your elders."

Seated in front of an empty fireplace was a bent old man in his eighties. He sat far forward, holding tight to the arms of his soft black chair. "We still haven't been able to do anything about age," he said to Thad. "I have a whole lab full of half-wits, overpaid half-wits, working on the problem."

Lon said, "Defense work pays better."

"We even have half-wits in the family now," said JP Walbrook.

"It's," said Thad down at the old man, "good to see you again, Johnny."

"Is it?" The old man studied Thad's face. "If only I . . . well, so you're back, Bob? I apologize for the imposition of yet more tests today. Dr. Rosenfeld's told us most of your story, and of course I had it thoroughly checked by my security people. Still I'd like to hear the details from you."

"Dr. Rosenfeld actually knows more than I do," began Thad. "Apparently, I don't quite know how yet, I woke up when the rioting destroyed the vaults in Grosse Pointe. I have a feeling a couple other guys who were stored there did, too. Most likely the awakening mechanisms got activated somehow during all that chaos." He shook his head, which was now a very good replica of the real Robert I's. "From then on until a few months ago . . . I'm not very clear. I must have wandered around from place to place, not knowing who I was."

"Yes," said the old man, "we were always afraid of that. The storage affecting, at least temporarily, the memory cells of the brain."

"Only temporarily, fortunately," echoed Dr. Rosenfeld from behind the old man's big black chair. "He began to remember who he was five months ago and——"

"I went to a doctor," said Thad. "I was living in a ghetto area known as Cleveland, Ohio, when I started getting glimpses, pieces of memory coming back. I knew a doctor who was working with the down-and-outs, a man I could trust with what I figured at the time might only be some kind of delusions."

"Fortunately," said Rosenfeld, "the the doctor was a man I know."

"All those conventions you hit do pay off, Doc."

"This colleague contacted me," continued Dr. Rosenfeld. "I began to do some checking, finally went out to Cleveland myself. I told no one in the the family at first. I wanted to be relatively certain this this young man was actually Robert B. Walbrook I. As as you know, Mr. Walbrook, I made numerous tests before I even—"

"Yes, I saw all that material, Rosenfeld," cut in JP. "And, Bob, what about the leukemia?"

"You remember, Johnny, we didn't know what all the side effects of the pseudodeath process would be," said Thad. "There seems to have been a total remission."

"That's true, as I reported to you," reminded the doctor.

"Glory be, " said Lon, "a miracle. And we're not even certain Walbrook Enterprises had anything to do with it."

"It's also possible," said Thad, "I got some kind of treatment during that long, blank, wandering period. I'm not sure."

"Lon, you and your sister can leave us now," ordered the old man in a slow voice. "You as well, Doctor."

When the three were gone, Thad sat down on the floor in front of the fireplace. It was a characteristic Robert I posture.

The old man continued to watch him. At last he said, "You can have your old rooms in the first house again." He held out his dry, freckled hand. "Welcome home, Bob."

Thad surveyed the oval white dining room. "Standards haven't slipped that much in fifty years," he said, inclining his head in the direction of Lyle Gunder. "I have no intention of eating with the help."

Gunder's lucite chair whapped into the wall, so forceful was his abrupt rising up. "Listen, you spurious son of a bitch!"

Thad gave him an annoying Bobby Walbrook grin. "Out, Gunder." He remained on the threshold of the large, spotless room.

The other members of the family, except for old JP, were already seated around the floating table.

Alex moved his servobox a few inches across the table top. "We . . . uh . . . didn't realize you'd be joining us for dinner . . . uh . . . Father. Somehow we had the impression you'd be resting up and—"

"I rested for half a century," Thad told him. "I'm back. I intend to take part in everything. Get out, Gunder."

The blocky man made a snarling sound, rubbing a fisted hand hard across his cheek. "I dine with the family," he said in a tightly controlled voice. "It's part of the accepted procedures laid down by—"

"It *was*." Thad came into the room.

"Uncle Robert," said the lovely JeanAnne, "you oughtn't to get yourself upset by—"

Thad laughed. "You'll all have to get used to the fact that I'm not quite as infirm as Johnny." He approached the glowering government agent. "They'll fix you up something in the Subsidiary Dining Room."

"We don't use the Sub for eats anymore, unc," said Lon. "It's a meeting room now."

"Be that as it may, there's bound to be some place for surly spies to chow down," said Thad.

"Don't push your luck, bastard," warned Gunder. "When I get the goods on you I'll—"

"Enough." Thad took hold of Gunder's arm. "Leave us."

"Don't you try to—"

Thad spun him around, delivered two chops to the side of his neck.

Gunder gagged, buckled, made a sloppy genuflection on the floor. He started to topple over.

Thad booted him in the backside, propelling the man into the smooth white wall. Before Gunder recovered from that, Thad caught him by the back of the tunic and dragged him to the arched doorway.

Badjett was lurking there. "Sir?" he said, eying the stunned Gunder.

"Show Mr. Gunder to one of the other kitchens." Thad returned to the dining area. There were three empty places around the floating table. He took the chair at the table's head.

"Bravo," said Lon. "You have an interesting style of combat, unc."

Thad said, "I picked up a few helpful tricks during my wanderings, apparently."

Cornelia said, "Meals will be much more pleasant without that lout in attendance. Now if we could only get back to the custom of wine with meals."

"Let's not break too much new ground all at once," said Lon.

The dark-haired JeanAnne was seated nearest to Thad. Despite the cautionings of Dr. Leader, Thad continued to find the girl attractive. "I hope my display of temper didn't unsettle you, JeanAnne," he said.

"Compared to some of the things that happen at a typical Walbrook family dinner . . . well, let's simply say I'm not unsettled."

"Go ahead and order, unc," suggested Lon. "You're the guest of honor."

Thad placed a hand on his servobox. Before he could punch out an order a buzzing shock shot up through his arm. "Hey!"

"Something wrong with that one," said Lon. "Why don't you use anoth——"

"I can fix this one." The box had been doctored. "These things have changed considerably since my day, but I think I can . . . sure, the anode's sitting cockeyed. There. This is one of our WE models, isn't it?"

"What else?" said Lon.

"I don't like to think of our customers getting a jolt."

"Oh, it livens up the dinner hour."

Cornelia concentrated on punching out her order. Then she said, "I was thinking today about the very first robot toy animal you built for me, Uncle Bobby. I think I still have it out in one of the storage pavilions someplace."

"A pony, wasn't it?" asked Lon.

Cornelia hesitated a second before saying, "Yes. His name was Pinto."

A serving robot came rolling in from the kitchen with a tray held in its three chrome hands. "Your dinner, Missy Cornelia."

Thad frowned. "I don't like that accent of his. Whose idea was that?"

"Guilty," said Lon. "But we were talking about that pony. Old Paint."

"Pinto," corrected Cornelia, watching the robot set her meal out before her.

"What I built for you, Muffin, was an elephant," Thad said. "You wouldn't have settled for anything as prosaic as a pony. And the elephant's name was Boswell."

JeanAnne, slowly, ordered her dinner. "You have my permission to toss Lon out along with Gunder, Uncle Robert," she said to Thad. "His little traps and snares are awfully heavy-handed."

"Aw, now, sis," said her brother. "We can't all be as subtle and witty as . . . which one was it? I can't remember whether you married that TV gunslinger or only—"

"You haven't ordered dinner, Lon," said Thad. "A dynamo like yourself needs plenty of food."

Lon punched at his servobox without looking at it. "We'll have to take a real look at the grounds tomorrow, unc. I imagine you're anxious to see your hydroponic greenhouses again."

"My greenhouse was of the more conventional kind, Lon. And Johnny tore it down soon after I fell ill."

"Oh, yeah. What could I have been thinking of?"

The serving robot reappeared with a tray for JeanAnne. "Dinner plenty hot, missy."

The girl watched Thad for a moment. "What was it like when you were wandering, Uncle Robert? Before you found your way back to us."

Thad grinned at her. "Is this another test?"

"No, I'm really curious," she said.

So he told her.

CHAPTER 7

They came marching through the snow, another batch of them. All about the same size, except for the long Negro on the end. All dressed in seamless tan business suits and all-season, see-through, executive-style ponchos.

Up in the gray morning sky somewhere another aircruiser sounded, approaching the landing field to the south of the salt-box complex. Down the main road toward House 1 a plum-colored landcar was rolling.

They were in the connecting tubes, too. Moving in clusters of two and three between the houses. Few of them allowed to go as far as House 6 and old JP.

Thad stepped back from the high windows of his study, away from his view of the coming and going Walbrook Enterprises executives.

A light tapping began on his door. "Come in," he called, starting toward the white door.

A knee-high, silver-plated syncaf machine came waddling along beside him, offering him a fresh cup, sloshing it slightly.

Thad accepted the hot syncaf, dismissed the fat little mechanism. "Good morning, Muffin," he said.

Cornelia Walbrook was standing in the doorway, a stack of information cartridges cupped in her knobby hands. "By the way, it's not really still golden, Uncle Bobby," she said.

"Your hair?"

"Yes, I have to use one of our WE oral dyes, Drink-Yourself-Blonde ✗2, to keep it looking this way."

"I'm glad you have." He set his cup on the edge of his bronze desk, took the cartridges from her. "Reminds me of the way things were before I left."

"The only trace of the simple sweet child I was then . . . oh, for Christ's sake, get away from me!"

The coffee machine had waddled over to the thin woman's side and was rubbing against her legs, a steaming cup of syncaf held up in one of its six tiny silver hands.

Cornelia kicked at the urn section with one booted foot. "I wish to God the old man didn't have the damn servos all set not to dispense any kind of sensible drinks until the cocktail hour. Go away, shoo, you overgrown coffeepot."

The syncaf machine persisted.

Thad was sorting through the information cartridges, putting them into separate piles atop the bronze desk. "Internal Cosmetics, External Cosmetics, Intellect-Expanding Toys, Non-Expanding Toys, Near Food, External Cosmetics, Near Food, Internal Cosmetics," he muttered as he sorted. "Although this is my third day here, I still haven't any idea what we've been doing for the United States Government all these years, or for any other government."

"Oh, very well, a half cup then," Cornelia said, hunching toward the machine. "Now, scat." She took a very careful sip of syncaf, her nose flexing. "Our WE brand of syncaf always manages to taste like last week's liver bile.

But then there must be a market for last week's liver bile or we wouldn't do so damn well selling this swill. What were you asking me, Uncle Bobby, before this contraption started molesting me?"

"I want," said Thad, strolling back toward the windows, "to get myself filled in on everything Walbrook Enterprises is doing. I realize it's going to take some time before I'm familiar enough with the current WE setup to take a full, active part in management again. Still and all, I'd like to cover the most important aspects first." Another carload of Walbrook executives was unloading out on the parking circle. These were all Chinese this bunch, and looked sleepy. "So far, all the material you and Lon and Alex have turned over to me, while interesting and moderately important, hasn't had anything to do with the major WE functions. Neither has the sleepbriefing stuff I get by night."

"In fifty years," said Cornelia, "JP has become used, extremely used, to running everything. As pleased as he is to have you back, Uncle Bobby, he isn't going to rush you into sharing complete control with him."

Thad turned to watch the thin woman. "How much influence does this guy Gunder have on Johnny?"

"Considerable," she answered. "It's quite possible he's persuaded old JP to be cautious until . . ."

"Until what?"

Her raised cup masked her mouth as she spoke. "I don't think Mr. Gunder quite accepts you as the real Robert B. Walbrook I."

"I am, though."

Slowly Cornelia said, "I don't know."

"You mean, you think . . . ?"

"It's so long ago," she said. "Perhaps those fifty years you slept had some effect on your overall character. You look like the Uncle Bobby I remember, and you have his charm and his sense of humor, but . . ."

"But?"

"I'm not exactly certain. I seem to sense you're too nice inside, almost gentle, to be one of us."

Thad said, "The years I wandered, Muffin, probably took some of the nastiness out of me."

"Oh, you were never openly nasty as I remember," she went on, eyes half closed. "Not the way JP can be, and my brother Bob. But yet . . . oh, Christ, forget it, Uncle Bobby. Not being able to get one damn servo to fix you a drink until practically nightfall gets on my nerves sometimes."

"You didn't mention Gilbert, my late brother. He had some splendid negative qualities as I recall." None of the Opposition Party digging had provided anything tangible about the accidental death two years ago of Gilbert Walbrook.

"He was pleasant, usually. Also, God bless his soul, handy enough to be able to job these Goddamn machines when he wanted to. I spent many happy afternoons with him until they . . ." She let the sentence die. "I'd best leave you to your catching up, Uncle Bobby."

"Until they what?"

The thin woman shook her head, left the room.

A moment later Lyle Gunder looked in around the still open door. "You got time to pack up and get the hell out," he said. "I can give you an hour, keep all the guards and dogs off your tail."

"You'll be out on your ass long before I am," said Thad.

"Ha," replied the big TSA agent. "I've got several little surprises in the works for you, Uncle Bob. Keep on your toes."

The syncaf machine was waddling toward Gunder when he pulled the door shut.

CHAPTER 8

It was two more days before Thad got a chance to prowl. Christmas Eve and everyone seemed preoccupied. From the windows of his suite in the original house, he could see the snow falling heavier down through the darkness, swirled by a harsh wind. He left his floating see-through chair and hurried across the room.

Only silence in the hallway. He moved quietly sideways out through the doorway. So far, none of the material on Walbrook Enterprises he'd been given to go through had contained one mention of the Hellhound Project. Today all the microcards, information cartridges, and wordspools had dealt with the pharmaceutical division of WE.

Since they weren't bringing any defense and weaponry material to him, Thad decided he'd go looking for it on his own. He got safely down to the foyer. He could hear the kitchen robots now, laughing and rattling, joking with the imported android French chef.

Thad let himself into the tube-tunnel leading to House 2. He'd seen Gunder take off in a family aircruiser at twilight, so he wouldn't have to worry about the bulky TSA agent.

The blue corridor leading to the file rooms was dimly lit

with hanging twists of light strip. Seasonal music was flowing out of the tiny speakers planted along the floor.

"Very festive," said Thad. He pushed open a door marked File Room A.

It was long and narrow and smelled of metal. Two walls were made up of metal-doored cubicles. At the rear was a row of retrieval machines and six four-legged microreaders.

That had been briefed by OP on how all these mechanisms worked. He located the central index box, which was built into the wall behind the retrieval machines. Squatting, since the control panel was set in low, he studied the face of the box. "The Hellhound stuff may not be stored in this room," he thought to himself, "but I should at least be able to find out where it is."

He was reaching out for the punch-buttons when something touched the back of his neck.

"Nobody should work on the night before Christmas."

It was JeanAnne, dark and pretty, standing with one warm hand outstretched. He grinned up at her. "You move very circumspectly."

"I guess I do. I saw you heading this way from my room," she said. "I wanted to invite you to see the tree get trimmed."

"Aren't all the trees decorated by now?"

"We always leave the one in the living room in House 2 here for tonight," said the girl. "It's an old family custom."

"Relatively old," said Thad, starting to rise.

JeanAnne slid a hand under his arm. "Let me help you, Uncle Robert."

"Hey. Even though I was born nearly eighty years ago, I'm not really too feeble."

The girl let go, smiling. "You're my great-uncle, though. I can't help thinking of great-uncles as venerable old souls. A lifetime of conditioning."

"I'm probably one of the few youthful great-uncles around," admitted Thad as they left the file room.

"Word is getting out, by the way, about you," said JeanAnne. "Inquiring people from the Conglomerate News Network, the *Fairpress* and *TimeLife* have been knocking at the gates."

"All to be turned away?"

"Oh, yes. Grandfather doesn't like interviews of any kind, and you . . . well, you he wants to handle especially carefully."

The living room of House 2 was lit only by globes of pale orange light floating up near the domed ceiling. In the center of the room stood a six-foot-tall Christmas tree, its strong pine smell filling the big room.

Thad asked, "One of ours?"

"Yes, a Walbrook nearwood long-life tree. You can tell by the smell, too piney to be real."

"I haven't gotten to our lumber business yet."

Christmas carols started up in the far corner of the room. Three tank-shaped, chest-high robots whirred across the room to circle the tree. One robot carried a basket stuffed full of tinsel, another held long twisting chains of realistic-looking holly, and the third a carton of nearglass bulbs.

"I thought we were going to decorate it," said Thad.

"No, Grandfather always thought children get too exuberant and noisy with jobs such as this," explained the girl. "So he had these servos built to take care of it. They've been with the family almost as long as I can remember. We can sit on the sofa there to watch."

"Careful, careful, children," warned one of the robots as they passed the tree. "Don't come too close; don't touch."

"Very cheerful." Thad eased down onto a see-through sofa filled with blue-tinted water and restless tropical fish. "How long have you been back with the family?"

"This time?" She sat close to him, both knees tight together and pointed toward him. "Oh, something like six months. Every once in a while I get married and then later I come home." She folded her arms under her small breasts. "A very dull chronicle it makes, my life. Tell me about . . . what was it like, being asleep all those years?"

"Tinsel last," said a robot as it began to twine holly on the pine-scented tree.

"It was simply like that," he said, "like being asleep."

"Did you dream?"

Thad thought. "No," he said finally.

JeanAnne hugged herself tighter. "How awful. It really is like being dead."

"The next best thing," he answered grinning. "Do you get much involved in the various family enterprises?"

"Me? Oh, some, but I—"

"Hum." Badjett had drifted into the room. He coughed again, his glistening metal hand shielding his mouth. "We have had word Mr. Robert II will definitely arrive shortly."

"Good," said the girl. "It'll be pleasant to have Dad

home on Christmas. He's almost always away someplace else on holidays."

Badjett turned his pink face toward Thad. "Mr. John suggests you join him in House 6 for a short business meeting in one half hour, sir. Mr. Lon and Mr. Robert II, fresh from his tour of South America, will also attend."

"Won't my son be there?"

"Mr. Alex is often not invited to these meetings, sir," said the cyborg butler. "His restlessness sometimes annoys Mr. John."

"I see."

"May I bring you an appropriate drink for the evening?" Badjett asked. "I must add, Miss JeanAnne, I am under strict orders not to serve you anything of a strong nature."

"Oh, an eggnog then."

"Same," said Thad. After the butler left, he asked Jean-Anne, "Who decides what you can have?"

"Grandfather now," she replied. "It's my father's idea actually. They both have the notion that if I hadn't been drinking so much at the time of my first marriage, it never would have happened." She unfolded her arms, clapped her hands together. "I've really had some fouled-up stretches of my life. I don't suppose you can understand that."

"I can," Thad told her.

A little over a half hour later he was up in the study of JP Walbrook. A new fire was getting going in the fireplace. You could still see the Walbrook Enterprises monogram on the pseudologs. The old man sat as he had the last time Thad had seen him, clutching tight to the chair arms as though he were afraid of pitching over to the floor.

Lon, holding a steaming cup of rum grog, was strutting back and forth in front of the high windows. "Pop's coming home for the holidays, unc," he said as Thad crossed the room. "It will be very gala. Maybe we can have one of the robots festoon him with mistletoe." He squinted through a window at the darkness. "Ah, I think I see the festive red and green lights of his aircruiser fast approaching now."

Old JP asked Thad, "How have you been coming with your backgrounding, Bob?"

"Considering I have to fill myself in on fifty years, not bad," Thad answered. "I haven't come across anything pertaining to our defense business, though. That and some of our other big activ—"

"We'll inform you on those aspects soon," promised the old man. "In fact, we may get into some facets of our government work tonight."

"Now you're back in the fold, unc, maybe you can help us cure Gramps of the habit of holding these meetings of his right before dinner," suggested Lon.

"We used to have them before breakfast," said Thad.

Lon made a slurping sound over his cup. "Just so I don't miss the plum pudding tonight."

The door opened. A tall, thin man, bald and slightly stooped, walked into the room. He was shrugging out of an all-season flying jacket. "Good evening, Father."

"You've been informed of the good news," the old man said. "We've located Bob, after all these years."

The bald man took three steps in the direction of Thad, then he stopped and shook his head. "This man isn't Robert Walbrook I," he said.

CHAPTER 9

The old man was out of his chair, pacing the room in a slow, crooked way. Thad had been asked to wait downstairs. Stopping near the high windows, he reached out one bony hand to touch the glass. "The winters get colder each year," he said. "What do you mean by what you said, Robert?"

His bald son hesitated. "I merely lost control of myself, Father." He was standing, slightly bent, with his back to the fireplace. "You know, travel shock, the holiday tensions . . . I blurted out the first thing which came to my mind when I saw him."

"You were a small boy when Bob had to be put away," reminded JP. He gradually turned. "Stop tapping that mug against your teeth, Lon."

"Sorry, Gramps." Lon had taken the old man's chair and was sitting in it sideways, his legs swinging over one arm of it. "Family squabbles always excite me."

"What makes you say he isn't Bob?" the old man asked his son.

Placing his palm against his forehead and then sliding it up onto his scalp, Robert II answered, "I don't know exactly, Father. There's something about him, I'm not certain what. He struck me on first glance as being . . . well, not a Walbrook."

"Doesn't have our thoroughbred look, huh, Pops?"

"In a way that is what I mean, yes."

"I'm aware of all the reasons an impostor might have for wanting to be taken for my brother." JP coughed a dry cough. "You don't imagine I allowed him to come here without looking into everything first?"

"No, I realize what was done by way of investigation," said Robert II. "I went carefully over all the memos and videograms you sent me, Father."

The old man's head was ticking up and down as he watched the whirling snow. "He checks out on every point. We've gone into the story and it all turns out true, the wanderings, the time in Cleveland. And Dr. Rosenfeld ran an incredible number of checks on him before bringing him here to us. Fingerprints, retinal patterns . . . everything matches."

Robert II said, "According to Dr. Rosenfeld."

"That hulking Gunder has also run numerous tests," the old man said. "That is all in addition to the independent checks I had made."

"Many things can be falsified," said Robert II. "Most of Uncle Robert's detailed medical records are lost it seems. So we have no—"

JP insisted, "It's much harder to fake his memories, his attitudes, the way he walks and talks. It's all as I remember him."

"From fifty years ago, Father, from another century."

"You'll find, should you reach an age comparable to

mine, Robert, that the early years of your life become clearer not dimmer as you reach this end of your life."

Robert II rubbed his bare head again. "You'd like this to be him. You've missed him, all these years . . . while he was in the vault and afterward when we thought he was dead."

"Yes, I've missed Bob," admitted JP. "There aren't many like him around anymore. But, Robert, I've never made a decision or a judgment on emotion. This man is my brother and—"

"So you're going to take him completely into the fold, Gramps," said Lon. "Let him help you run things."

"I intend to, yes," said the old man. "That's only fair. It was what Bob and I agreed to back when he submitted to the pseudodeath business. It's what the law says is fair."

Robert II said, "Certainly, Father. Let's, however, be cautious. . . . Let's be absolutely certain he is Robert B. Walbrook I."

"I am certain."

"Lyle Gunder is running his own check, using all the Total Security Agency facilities, Father. Nothing will be lost if we wait for the results of all that."

"What do you mean wait?"

"I think Pop means we can still toss a few fatted calves unc's way," suggested Lon. "We ought to hold off, though, on letting him in on all the family secrets."

"Yes, exactly," said Robert II. "I think that would be an excellent approach to the problem, Father."

"I don't see Bob's return as a problem." The old man pressed his fingers to the dark glass of the window. "And we have been exposing Bob very gradually to the current workings of Walbrook Enterprises. To please you, Robert, we will be even more cautious than we have been."

"Thank you, Father."

CHAPTER 10

They didn't try to kill Thad until the day after Christmas.

Just after lunch he was in his rooms in House 1, working in the study which had been Robert Walbrook I's. Old JP, as well as the newly returned Robert II, had provided him with even more background material. Several cartons of microcards, bundles of faxcopies, but still nothing at all about Hellhound.

His television set out in the living room suddenly turned itself on. "Ladies and gentlemen, the President of the United States."

"My friends," said Warren Parkinson in his nervous voice, "there's nothing to get excited about. I really only . . . well, I like to talk to the American people now and then. As the President of the United States, not to mention being Commander in Chief of the Armed Forces, I have a perfect right. I mean, I can come on and say, 'Hello there,' to my people any old time I want. Well, actually . . . one thing is sort of bothering me. I keep hearing talk about my health . . . what was it Mr. Reisberson of our illustrious Washington *Post-Star* called me? 'A nervous twitch,' I believe. 'That nervous twitch in the White House,' I believe is how he put it."

Thad walked into the living room, tried to turn off the set. It wouldn't allow that.

"I mean to say," continued the President, licking his lips, "I only last week had a complete, really head-to-toe, physical. I'm, and here I'm quoting the Surgeon General himself, I'm in 'shipshape.' Look, I even brought you copies of my X-rays and my electrocardiograms and my brain-wave recordings to look at. Well, admittedly the old brain does show a slight . . ."

Thad's pixphone rang.

"Hello?"

JeanAnne appeared on the small square phone screen. "Care to take a walk, uncle? Or are you glued to the President."

"A walk would be fine, my child."

"Oh, am I still addressing you as though you were venerable? Forgive it. I'll see you out behind House 2 in five minutes."

On his way downstairs Thad encountered Alex on the staircase.

"Oh . . . uh . . . hello, Father," said the lanky man, attempting a smile. He had his arms full of bundles of faxmemos neatly tied. "I was just . . . uh . . . coming to talk with you."

"What about, Alex?"

The son of Robert I shrugged his narrow shoulders. "Nothing . . . uh . . . important. It can wait if you . . ."

"I promised JeanAnne I'd take a stroll with her. Drop in later, though."

"I'd like to, yes. I hardly get to see you. They don't allow me into many of the . . . uh . . . top-level meetings, you know. And they . . . uh . . . they're going to keep you . . ." He turned the sentence into a cough, closed his mouth on it.

"Going to keep me what?"

"I ought not to . . . but . . . uh . . . you are my father after all," said the lank Alex in a low voice. "I'm not supposed to . . . uh . . . know this, but I find things out. It's been decided to keep you out of the . . . uh . . . top-priority things until . . . uh . . . until everyone is satisfied."

Thad grinned. "So the Gunder view of me is shared around the old homestead?"

"Not by me, Father," Alex told him. "But I'm afraid . . . well, you'll be wanting to get to JeanAnne. You're certain it . . . uh . . . won't bother you if I pop in on you later?"

"Not at all," Thad assured him.

JeanAnne was already outside when Thad got there. Wearing an all-season hiking suit of black and scarlet, a small scarlet cap on her head. "Usually I like to walk up through the woods, up toward the hills over there."

"I think I'm up to that."

"Let's proceed then, uncle." She took his hand, leading him away from the complex of salt-box houses.

The day was chill and clear, the thin sunlight tinting the snow a pale yellow. "Our President seemed particularly twitchy today," remarked Thad.

"You've been away. He was almost serene compared to—"

"I'm a little unsettled by the fact we're doing so much work for the government. With a guy like Parkinson in charge. Of course, so far I don't have a very clear picture of the defense end of Walbrook Enterprises."

"You're not supposed—" began JeanAnne. She took her hand out of his, touching her fingertips to her cheek.

"Not supposed to be told?"

The girl looked away. "Will you allow me to tactfully change the subject, uncle? I'm sorry."

"Sure." Increasingly since he'd been here the idea of trying to get information from the girl bothered him. The Opposition Party might not like it, but there it was. He began talking about other things.

When they were ten minutes into the oaks and maples a crunching sound commenced off to the right.

"Don't let it bother you," JeanAnne said when she noticed him turning his head. "It's Chambers-26 probably."

"And who's he?"

"Or it might be Chambers-25. Grandfather keeps two of them stationed in this part of the forest," she explained. "Robots, as you might imagine. It's an Old World touch really; they're gamekeepers. Designed to look after the wild life and keep off poachers."

"Do we get many poachers?"

"Not since I can remember. Mostly Chambers-25 and Chambers-26 take care of feeding the squirrels and the chipmunks and birds in the winter. Occasionally they shoot a rat."

The crunching grew louder. All at once Thad's back began to feel strange, as though he had a big X drawn between his shoulder blades. He glanced over his shoulder. "Down!" he shouted as he pushed JeanAnne over into the snow.

The big robot's first shot missed Thad, sizzled the dry bark off a dark oak trunk.

Thad was on the ground, rolling away fast in the snow.

The mechanism had a blaster rifle built into its right arm. The weapon crackled again. The snow two feet to the left of Thad melted, splashing him with great drops of boiling water.

He kept on rolling, got up and dived around behind another thick oak.

"Stop it, Chambers!" JeanAnne was crying.

Hunched low, Thad went running through the trees, circling over the hard-packed snow. He got himself behind the big slow-moving mechanism. The robot wore a thick red mackinaw, and nothing else, over its chrome-plated body. And for some reason a pair of earmuffs were stuck on its thick head.

Thad shinnied up a tree directly to the rear of the thing.

The gamekeeper must have heard that. It began slowly to turn.

Thad was in the air, hurling himself toward it. Both his booted feet slammed hard into the robot's back.

There was an enormous clanging thud. The gun hand went off once more, burning up brush, splashing hot snow. Then the big gamekeeper tottered, toppled forward.

Thad went for the mechanism's head, jumping up and down. Cracking and smashing sounded beneath his boots.

Chambers, whichever one this was, 25 or 26, gave a flap of the arms. A smell of burning plastic began to spew out of his ears.

"Uncle Robert," said JeanAnne, "you can stop; he's . . . dead, or whatever you call it with machines."

Thad had driven the machine's bright head far down into the hard snow. He stepped back and away, wiping at his face. "Don't tell me that bastard mistook me for a poacher."

"I can't understand what happened." She was still kneeling in the snow where he'd shoved her. She held out a slender hand to him.

He stood watching her for a few seconds before helping her up. "Somebody," he said.

"What?" She brushed away snow.

Thad shook his head, saying, "Probably a malfunction. Yeah, I'm sure that will turn out to be the explanation. We'd better get inside before the other one makes a try."

"Other one?"

"You told me there were two of them, 25 and 26," said Thad. "Which one was this?"

JeanAnne turned her face toward the sprawled machine. "I can't tell now," she said.

Gunder was in the center of the octagonal room surrounded by blue-smocked technicians. Sensing Thad's arrival in Lab 3, he turned. "How's the girl?"

"Fine. We're both fine."

The remains of the smashed gamekeeper robot were spread out on a floating lucite medtable. The mechanism's red mackinaw had been sliced away and lay crumpled on the neotile floor.

"What went wrong with him?" Thad asked as he approached the cluster of technicians.

"Malfunction," replied two of them at once.

"A simple malfunction, so they say," Gunder said. "No need for you to hang around, phony."

Ignoring him, Thad pushed up to the floating table. "Can I look him over?"

"Of course, sir," said three of the technicians.

Thad had been turned into a fair technician himself. He checked over the defunct robot thoroughly. "Guess you're right," he said finally. He left the table, started for the lab door.

Gunder trotted after him. "You couldn't find anything wrong?"

"Nope."

"If that bozo had knocked you off, I wouldn't be crying in my maltz over you," the large agent said. "Still the girl is sort of cute . . . and I'm always a little suspicious when an accident happens around this place."

"I'm not saying this was an accident," said Thad. "I couldn't find anything to prove it wasn't. If that robot was doctored, he's been doctored back again."

Grunting, Gunder said, "One more reason for you to scram while you can. Maybe next time you'll have an accident you can't walk away from." He raised his hand to slap Thad on the back.

"Don't," suggested Thad.

CHAPTER 11

The paramedical robot handed Thad back his clothes. It gave a negative shake of its ball-shaped head before rolling out of the white metal room.

"Bend over a little farther," suggested Dr. Rosenfeld. "Um, yes, everything seems to be just fine, Mr. Walbrook."

"They wouldn't have been able to plant a mike in there without my knowing." Thad straightened up, began dressing.

"You you're not supposed to say anything relevant until I give you the key phrase," the grizzled physician reminded. "Yes, Mr. Walbrook, you're in the pink of condition. That's the phrase." He slipped off his synthskin glove and crossed to let the wall sanitizer work on his hands. "And don't get overconfident about where and where where not they can hide a bug on you or your clothes. Obviously obviously somebody out there on the estate is suspicious of you."

"Okay, we can talk now." The short, stocky Crosby Rich of the Opposition Party came into the examination room eating a kelp donut.

"I'll attend attend to my other patients."

When Dr. Rosenfeld was out in the corridor, Rich said, "A dumbbell. So they tried to knock you off, huh?"

"Yep." Thad seamed his tunic. "Somebody did."

"Rosenfeld tells me you've been doing a good job fooling the Walbrook tribe so far," said Rich. "Where'd you screw up?"

"Wait now," Thad said. "If somebody is suspicious I'm not the real Robert, why not simply call my bluff? Unmask me in public, in front of old JP."

"If they've got you figured for a spy, they may want to get rid of you quickly and permanently. I'm not sure."

"It could also be there are Walbrooks with purely personal reasons for wanting to do me in. The same reasons that may have caused brother Gilbert's accident."

"You haven't found out anything about those fatal accidents the family members keep having?"

"No, it's one of the topics we don't talk about."

"You said, in one of the reports Rosenfeld smuggled out, that Robert II openly accused you of being a fake."

Sitting in a white metal chair, Thad said, "Yeah, that he did. I get the impression the old man talked him out of the notion. Why Robert ※2 said it, I don't yet know. At any rate, they still haven't completely accepted me."

"Robert ※2 would like you to be fake," said the OP man. "Before you showed up there was only one rickety old dumbbell between him and complete control of the whole works."

Thad said, "And this Total Security guy, Gunder, is still checking up on me."

"We know about Gunder. So far, all the pieces of your phony background that we planted are holding up." He took an angry bite out of the kelp donut. "There is one thing, though. We think Gunder's been able to get a lead on some old medical records of the authentic Robert I. These could include things like a brain-wave recording."

Thad poked his tongue under his upper lip to produce a popping sound. "Then I should get out of there even sooner than planned."

"We may be able to sidetrack Gunder. But a little extra swiftness wouldn't hurt," said Rich. "Haven't you got anything on the Hellhound Project?"

"Not as much as a mention," answered Thad. "I gather from Alex there's a gentlemen's agreement to keep most of the security stuff away from me until I've proven myself. And I can't keep asking after the defense stuff."

"I'm wondering why they don't quite accept you as the real thing."

"I told you, the old man does. It's Robert ⚹2 and Gunder who are plugging for second-class status for me, I think," said Thad. "Alex calls me Father."

"Another dumbbell." Rich finished the donut. "I only eat these things when I'm in a tense situation." He wandered over to a blank metallic wall, leaned with his back against it. "Rosenfeld tells me the girl was with you when the gamekeeper tried to pot you. Did she maybe set you up?"

"No."

"You sure?"

"She could have been killed herself. The damn machine was shooting all over the place."

"When they went over the robot, what did they find?"

"No evidence of tampering is the official story," said Thad. "I didn't see anything to prove otherwise."

Rich watched him for a few seconds. "You'd best keep remembering JeanAnne is your grandniece."

"I know who she is."

"Living with all your loved ones over the holidays has mellowed you, McIntosh," Rich told him. "You're not the same crusty son of a bitch I dragged up out of the lower depths of Manhattan a couple months ago."

"You turned me into sweet-tempered Bobby." Thad left his chair to walk toward the small OP man. "Don't worry about my judgment being screwed up, Rich."

"Okay, okay." Rich held his palms toward the approaching Thad. "Get back to the estate now and get us some results. You may—"

"I know," cut in Thad. "I may not have all that much time."

Nodding, Rich said, "We aren't certain what Lyle Gunder and his Total Security boys may come up with. Besides—"

"Somebody out there may try to kill me again."

CHAPTER 12

The second attempt came the following day.

Early in the afternoon Badjett tapped discreetly on the door of Thad's study with his aluminum fist. "Beg pardon, sir. Mr. John would like you to join him."

Pushing aside a fresh bundle of micrographs, Thad stood. "Sure, okay."

Badjett entered, holding out an all-season hiking jacket. "I think this will be suitable, Mr. Robert."

"Suitable for what?"

"Since the day is so mild, Mr. John is in the mood to spend some time out of doors, sir."

"I didn't know Johnny ever went out where he couldn't control the temperature." He allowed the cyborg butler to help him into his coat. "Where do I find him?"

"He will await you at the snowcar barn," replied Badjett. "You know where that is, I trust."

Thad grinned. "Yes, I do, Badjett. Just this side of our private lake."

He went downstairs, seaming up the jacket. Instead of heading immediately outside, Thad ducked into the connecting tunnel. "Old JP must have something pertaining to the Hellhound Project in his study," he said to himself as he jogged through the tinted tube. "Now's a good time to look."

Thad made it through House 2 and halfway along the sea-blue-tinted see-through tunnel linking it with House 3.

Then a loud rapping commenced on the wall of the tube.

Slowing, Thad looked to his left.

Alex was out there, an awkward smile touching his lean face. "Father," he said.

"Yes, what?"

"JP is . . . uh . . . waiting for you down there." He pointed one gloved hand back. "I . . . uh . . . just ran into him and he . . . uh . . . asked me to see what was keeping you." Alex's breath made fuzzy puffballs on the other side of the tunnel wall as he carefully yelled his words.

"I thought he wanted to meet me in his study." Thad returned to House 2 and let himself out into the day. By then Alex was gone.

The snow was soft underfoot, slightly muddy in color. The sun felt warm in the hazy afternoon air. Beside the big peak-roofed, red-synthwood barn the old man was standing alone, bent and resting one bony hand against the barn door.

"I've had them warm up my snowcar," said JP. "If you'll help me in, Bob, we can get started on a little ride."

The vehicle had narrow noryl skis on its underside and was the size of a small landcar. It had two passenger cockpits, both open and unshielded. "One of our own designs I see," said Thad as he boosted the old man into the rear seat. "Where to?"

"Nowhere in particular, Bob." JP buckled himself in.

"It's the feeling of swift movement and rushing air I enjoy."

Thad took the control seat, eased the snowcar out of the shadowy barn. He guided it along level ground, paralleling the wide frozen lake.

"I wanted to talk with you, Bob."

"Okay, do."

"If you've been feeling that I don't quite accept you or trust you," said the old man, "please try to understand it isn't because I don't believe in you. There are many pressures on me and—"

"Yeah, I know how it is, Johnny. Plus which, I remember how it was."

Nodding his head as they moved swiftly over the snow JP said, "Only this morning, Bob, I was wishing you were working more closely with me. There's a new outfit over in Japan, the Oyayubi Works, claiming they can produce the damping vanes for some of our household servos at a third of the cost of the Rotterdam plant we're contracted with now. What I'm wondering is, should everything they say test out true, is it worth switching. What would you say, offhand?"

"Well, offhand," began Thad. This was one of the toughest aspects of the impersonation. OP had processed him to look exactly like Robert B. Walbrook I, to act like him, to accurately imitate his grin and his mannerisms, even his voice. But to be able to think like the missing Robert wasn't something which could be taught, or sleep-briefed in, with much degree of certainty. "Offhand, Johnny, I'd say—"

The entire rear end of the snowcar, the engine end,

exploded. Jagged shards of plastic, twisted metal struts, chunks of the compact engine went splattering through the air. The controls jerked free of Thad as the remains of the machine careened down toward the ice-covered lake.

Thad grabbed the release on his safety belts, jumped up onto his seat, and flung himself clear. He hit the slushy snow on his right elbow and knee. His ankle wouldn't work the first time he tried to rise.

After three tries he got himself upright. He spun, went running toward the lake.

The snowcar seemed to be hanging in the air between the snowy ground and the lake. Its back side was nearly gone, a black, sooty tangle trailing streamers of harsh blue smoke.

The old man, still strapped in, was slumped far to the left.

Then the vehicle hit the ice, bounded twice, and went skidding in dizzy arcs. The sun-warmed ice groaned, began to crack.

Thad dropped down on his stomach, started to work his way out across the ice of the lake.

The snowcar was moving more slowly. It stopped entirely, some thirty feet from the shore.

Reaching the thing, Thad carefully pulled himself up by the runners.

JP was alive, but a fragment of the exploded car had torn a wide gash across the back of his head.

Thad ripped him free of the belts, hefted the old man out of the snowcar.

The ice cracked further, with a great wrenching sound.

Flat out again, Thad dragged JP back toward the white shore.

"I don't—" murmured the old man, "I don't . . . understand."

"Understand what?"

"The gamekeeper," he said. "The gamekeeper . . . malfunctioned. Now the snowcar. It's not . . . typical of Walbrook products. Not at all. I—" He passed over into unconsciousness as Thad got him safely onto solid ground.

CHAPTER 13

The silver serving robot glided forward to refill Thad's wine glass. "Allow-me-sir," it said through a tiny speaker horn mounted atop its shiny head.

"No, no more, thanks," he told the mechanism.

"Very-well-sir."

"I was about to offer a toast to you, unc," said Lon from the other end of the long peach-colored dinner table of Dining Room 2. "To your heroic rescue of Gramps."

"You ought . . . uh . . . not to make . . . uh . . . your little jokes while JP's lying over there in . . . uh . . . serious—"

"He's not all that hurt," Lon told Alex. "Dad was talking with Dr. Rosenfeld and Dr. Malley before I came down to dinner. Gramps isn't seriously—"

"Freshen-your-wine-sir?"

"Sure, pour away. Alex and I can go ahead with the toast. Since unc won't join us, and Aunt Muffin and sis aren't allowed."

"Accidents," said the gaunt Cornelia, across the table from her grinning nephew, "always happen to the wrong people."

JeanAnne was sitting next to Thad. In a low voice she said, "I'm glad you survived, Uncle Robert."

"I seem to be pretty good at surviving."

"Father had two of his best men from the Trumbull plant out to go over that snowcar," the girl said, her hair faintly glowing in the light of the floating globes of soft orange light. "They found absolutely—"

"Absolutely nothing wrong," Thad finished for her.

"Father told you?"

"I guessed."

JeanAnne's tongue inscribed a small circle on the inside of her cheek. "You think this was a second try for you, don't you?"

"The possibility occurred to me, yeah," he answered. "As a bonus, this time they would have got rid of Johnny, too."

Her hand, hidden by the table, drifted over to rest on his leg. "Grandfather's death," she said, "your death . . . they'd only benefit us. The rest of us in the family."

Thad nodded. "That might be why my brother Gil had his accident, too."

The hand tightened on his leg, then went away. "But, Uncle Robert, that was two long years ago. You don't believe one of us has been . . . planning things like that all this time?"

"Maybe longer."

"Ahem-ahem," said the serving robot who had appeared at Thad's right.

"Yes?"

"The-doctor-wishes-to-see-you-in-the-corridor."

"Excuse me," Thad said to the girl as he pushed back from the table.

Rosenfeld, scratching at his grizzled hair with both hands, was circling a claw-foot nearoak table in the hallway. "He wants to wants to talk with you, friend," he said to Thad.

"How is Johnny doing?"

"He's doing as well as can be expected."

"Which means?"

The doctor ceased scratching. "They didn't succeed in killing him. He'll live."

Close beside the doctor, Thad asked, "He suspects it wasn't an accident?"

"Sure sure he does, friend."

"Any specific person?"

"He doesn't trust trust any of them at this point," said Rosenfeld. "With the exception of you." His left eye fluttered on the brink of a wink. "Better get over to House 6 and see see him."

The neorubber cot floated three feet above the floor, just beyond the glow of the nearwood fire. Gesturing at the door with one gnarled hand, the old man said, "You can go get yourself some dinner now, Robert. Bob and I have a few things to talk over."

The bald Robert II was hunkered on a tin stool, watching his injured father. "I think it would be best if I—"

"Go away now," JP told him.

Thad was standing in front of the fireplace. When Robert II, after a slow-sighing rise, had left, Thad said, "You look to be in fair shape, Johnny."

An oval had been shaved on the back of the old man's

head. It was covered over with a white healing-patch and spread with synflesh. "That wasn't the intention," he said. "I was meant to die."

"I hear," said Thad, "they couldn't find any sign the snowcar had been fooled with."

"Couldn't, wouldn't," said the old man. "I have the impression someone, someone in our family, I'm afraid, has been working their way up a list. My name is at the top."

"Also mine, probably."

"Yes, they want both of us out of the way." Rising up enough to rest on one elbow, JP went on. "I have to conclude that Gil's death may also have been arranged."

"Any ideas, Johnny? As to who?"

The old man stared into the crackling fire. "Too many ideas," he replied. "However, Bob, this isn't the chief reason I want to talk to you tonight. I haven't discussed all of our activities with you thus far, so it's probable you aren't aware I was intending to travel, a thing I dislike increasingly as I age, to travel down to South America early next week."

"I didn't know that, no."

"Such a jaunt, according to both Rosenfeld and Malley, wouldn't be advisable for me now. Therefore, Bob, I'd like you to go."

"Okay, Johnny. Whereabouts in South America?"

"To Brazil, to New Rio," said the old man. "In view of what's happened, I feel it more sensible to trust you than some of the others around here. We'll operate that way from here on out." He slowly eased himself back down. "You'll be in New Rio to take a look at some tests, Bob."

"What are we testing?"

"Something called the Hellhound," said JP.

Blam! Blam!

"Has a certain certain low-class excitement, doesn't it?" said Dr. Rosenfeld.

"Nope," replied Thad.

They were sharing a one-way nearglass booth high up in the domed ceiling of the Westport Gunslinger Drome. Down on the pseudosawdust floor, teams of gunfighters were shooting it out with stunguns.

"Pitting pitting women gunslingers against men is is a stimulating idea," said the doctor. "Did did they have gunslinger stadiums in your day?"

"I'm younger than you, remember?"

"Oh, yes, that's right. I guess I'm falling falling under the spell of your impersonation. Which reminds me . . ." He opened the lycra medical bag which was resting on his knees. "I might as well give you your injection while we're waiting."

"What injection?"

Blam! Blam!

"My, um, look at the breasts breasts on that lady who's just now biting the dust," remarked Dr. Rosenfeld. "This is an extra booster for your Non-Self-Betrayal serum."

"What's wrong with the stuff you already shot into me?"

"Nothing nothing, but they'll be giving you multi-immune shots for your trip down to Brazil. Be a good good opportunity to try another talk-drug on you."

Rolling up his tunic sleeve, Thad asked, "What do you mean another talk-drug?"

"Your last urinalysis showed they'd used something on you." The doctor placed a parasite needle on Thad's arm, flicked it on. "I haven't haven't had a chance to mention it to you before this."

"We can assume, huh, my antibetrayal stuff was working?"

"That's the logical logical conclusion."

"You're getting closer," said Crosby Rich as he stepped into the booth. He held a plyowrapped sandwich in his hand.

Dr. Leader, hair especially upstanding today, came in after him. "Want to mention that you're jeopardizing your impression management, Thad."

"Want any of this?" Rich seated himself in a floating chair next to Thad and began unwrapping his sandwich. "It's simulated buffalo jerky on pseudo-7 grain. Has a catchy Old West sound to it, but—"

"What did I tell you about disrupting your performance by getting sentimental about your audience?" persisted Dr. Leader.

Blam! Blam!

Thad detached the needle from his arm, returned it to Rosenfeld. "This is some bon voyage party. I liked it better when we met in Rosenfeld's offices."

"This location is completely safe," Rich assured him. "Rance Keane is an OP supporter."

"Who's he?"

"Only the #1 gunslinger in America. Where have you

been? Never mind . . . do you know what the Hellhound
is?"

"It's a weapon."

"We knew that. What sort of weapon?"

"The sort that's going to be tested in New Rio in three
days."

"You mean to tell me that's all you know, even after the
old boy took you into his confidence?"

"He's in the process of taking me, I'm not all the way in
yet," explained Thad. "Apparently they're not going to
tell me anything else until I get out of the country."

"You may not get out of the country," warned Dr.
Leader. "No, you keep acting spoony about that underweight JeanAnne Walbrook and—"

"You mistake familial affection for something else,
Doc."

"Listen, you're almost at your goal, at *our* goal," said
Leader. "Don't go throwing it away because of—"

"Go away before I disrupt your performance."

After taking a careful bite of his jerky sandwich and
wincing, Rich said, "You're not really getting interested in
that girl? You've read her records. Why, she's had at least
a half dozen—"

"We're supposed to be meeting to work out procedures
for my stay in New Rio," reminded Thad. "My earlier rule
about sermons and pep talks still holds."

"Smitten," said Dr. Leader forlornly. "He's smitten with
that girl."

Blam! Blam!

"Good good show," said Dr. Rosenfeld, looking down
on the new round of gunfighting.

CHAPTER 14

"Ever been down here before, unc?"

Thad was sitting next to a window of the private Walbrook Enterprises autojet. It was early morning outside. "Back in the 20th century," he answered. "It wasn't New Rio then."

"All the wars of liberation here pretty much finished off this part of Brazil," said Lon. "New Rio they built on top of the ruins, proving there's hope for all of us. Right, sis?"

In the seat beside Thad the dark lovely JeanAnne said, "I'm starting to have doubts that applies to you."

Lon laughed. "You've been in New Rio before, haven't you, sis? On your first honeymoon as I recall, or was it the second? Were you in any shape to get an impression of—"

"Go up and sit with the robot again," Thad told him.

"Don't let our sibling kidding annoy you, unc." Lon shuffled along the thick airship carpeting to the door he'd just come through. "I came to tell you we'll be landing at our Walbrook field in ten minutes. Cheer up, sis."

"I have," JeanAnne said to Thad, "mixed feelings about this trip, uncle."

"Good thing you're along. Being alone in Brazil for a week with Lon—"

"Oh, I enjoy being with you." She smiled a quiet smile.

"It's simply that Lon has a way of . . . well, I do know why Grandfather wanted me to accompany you."

"Probably wants you to act as a bodyguard," said Thad, watching the girl's profile.

"Yes, he's been terribly concerned since the snowcar accident last week." She locked her hands together, hooked them over one knee. "I know they couldn't find anything wrong with the snowcar or with Chambers-26. . . ."

"It was 26 and not 25 then."

"Yes," she said, frowning. "Don't make it a joke. I'm worried, too. You could have been killed . . . twice. And Grandfather as well the last time."

"These accidents have had one positive result. Johnny has taken me completely into his confidence finally."

JeanAnne said, "I don't know if you'll be happy about what you're going to learn down here."

"I have to know everything Walbrook Enterprises is up to, which includes this Hellhound Project," said Thad. "What is it exactly?"

"You'll see when we get to our lab complex outside New Rio," said the girl. "Can we talk about something else now, please."

"Sports, literature, the theater? I'm still fifty years out of touch, but—"

The girl put her hand on his. "I'll tell you about the last time I was in New Rio."

A vast strip of formal garden stretched between the lab complex and the rim of the enormous one-way dome which shielded it. There was a jungle brightness all about, intensely green palms, scarlet blooms, great tangles of purple vine. Yellow butterflies flickered high above; multicolored birds called from the branches of high twisting trees.

Lon laughed, stretching up his arms. "This is what I call a slice of the good life, unc."

His eyes on the distant cluster of gray domes which made up the Walbrook lab complex, Thad said, "It's greener than Connecticut. Now when do we get a look at the Hellhound?" They'd been here nearly a half hour, Lon giving them a leisurely tour of the grounds.

"No rush, unc," said Lon. "Life in South America is paced differently, you know. I'll bet, sis, you found it even took longer to pick up—"

"I'd just as well go inside." JeanAnne was holding on to Thad's arm.

"In due time," chuckled her brother. "I thought we'd have a little refreshment out here." His fingers snapped.

Rustling sounded behind him.

Thad spun, shaking free of the girl.

It was only a silver waiter-robot, rolling toward them with a serving tray. The robot had a black mustache.

"Mustache is my idea," said Lon. "Latin touch, unc."

"Very sophisticated."

"This is real coffee." Lon took two cups off the tray, handing them to Thad and JeanAnne. "It's still legal in Brazil. Sorry I can't serve you anything harder, sis."

"You're much too jolly," the dark-haired girl said. "What do you—?"

"Nothing, sis, honest. It's simply that New Rio excites me." He took the third cup and dismissed the robot. "Carry on, Joaquim." He made an urging gesture with his hand. "Come along, folks, try this great authentic coffee." When they did, he nodded happily.

JeanAnne began to frown, listening. She moved to the edge of the mossy path, pushed aside some high yellow ferns. "Lon, these lab animals must have gotten loose."

"Oh, did they?"

In a small clearing, three small chimpanzees were huddled together near the bole of a tree.

"Probably only decorations." Lon slurped at his coffee.

"No, they aren't. See, they're wearing ID tabs on the ankles."

"Huh." Lon beckoned Thad. "What do you think, unc? Are these lab animals or what?"

Thad joined the others. "They look frightened."

"How can anyone, even a chimp, be afraid out here in this Eden?" asked Lon, laughing.

The chimpanzees grew more agitated now. They held on to each other, pushing back against the tree.

"The trouble with them," observed Lon, "is they know what's been happening to their buddies. So we're not going to get a pure surprise reaction. However . . ."

Thad felt something was approaching, but he didn't see or hear anything. Then, for an instant, he saw three tiny flashes of light over the clearing.

The chimps separated, began trying to climb up into the tree.

One of them got as high as the lowest branch. It gave a chittering scream, fell to the ground clutching itself. It died in midair.

The other two chimpanzees fell. They twitched for only a few seconds, evacuated and died.

"Oh, damn you, Lon." JeanAnne hit against him with one clenched fist. "Damn you." She turned, went running away from them.

Thad nodded at the dead chimps. "What did it?"

Lon replied, "What else? The Hellhound."

CHAPTER 15

The middle-sized Negro was holding it between thumb and forefinger. "I'm justifiably proud of it, my boy," he told Thad.

They were all in an oval room deep within the lab complex. The walls were tinted the same soft blue as Dr. E. Jack Nally's one-piece labsuit.

Thad walked a few steps closer to the black doctor. "So that's the Hellhound."

JeanAnne, pale, was leaning against a work table. "That's one of three types, isn't it?"

"Very good, dear girl," said Dr. Nally. "You're showing a much keener knowledge of our activities these days."

"She's between husbands, Prof," said Lon. "She's got more time to use the other end of her body."

Thad narrowed his eyes, studying the tiny copper-colored object in the lab director's hand. "Looks like a gnat."

"Yes, doesn't it?" agreed Dr. Nally. "A harmless little gnat." He let the tiny object roll down into his pink palm, closed his fingers over it. "Yet it is one of the most deadly antipersonnel weapons ever devised, if I do say so myself."

"How does it work?"

"This particular model seeks out body heat," explained

the amiable Dr. Nally. "In the demonstration you recently witnessed outdoors, my boy, a few adjustments were made, to make certain it sought out only the monks."

JeanAnne said, "That was most thoughtful."

"Don't be peevish, sis. There was also something in the coffee to give you temporary immunity to this particular model."

Dr. Nally tossed the Hellhound, caught it. "What you see here, my boy, is a perfect microminiaturized antipersonnel missile," he explained to Thad. "This particular model, to repeat, seeks out its victims by their body heat and then delivers a lethal shot of quick-acting nerve poison. Death usually supervenes within fifteen seconds."

"Kills with a sting," said Thad.

"Similar to a sting, but much more deadly," replied the black Nally. "Incidentally, on this new improved model we're running about 85% effective on kills.

"Hey, that's 14% better than the earlier model, Prof."

"Yes," smiled the lab head. "I'm sure it will be more than satisfactory to the Multi-Pentagon in Washington. They almost accepted the last model, until I talked them into renegotiating the contract and coughing up another quarter billion. I think everyone concerned is going to admit it was worth it, more than worth it."

Thad asked, "This is for battlefield use only?"

Dr. Nally's eyes clicked in the direction of Lon before he answered, "This one is, yes. You understand our own military personnel will be rendered immune to the Hellhounds. I have a miniaturized antimissile device, a spray-on repellent, and an oral repellent. Remind me to show those to you before you leave."

"The oral one was what I spiked our java with, unc," said Lon.

"I think the antimissile device, while the most costly of the three methods, affords the best protection," said the Negro scientist. "Now admittedly an enemy might come up with a countermeasure of his own. In wars such as we've been having lately, though, the enemy has usually been of a simple, uneducated sort. It isn't immediately likely they'd come up with anything to stop us. And should they, or their allies, why we can then—"

"There are other types of Hellhound?" asked Thad.

"Yes, my boy."

"How do they differ?"

Lon said, "Wait until tonight, unc. I'm arranging another little demo for you and sis over at our tower offices in the heart of New Rio. Can you make it?"

"I'll make it," said Thad.

CHAPTER 16

Thad walked into the tower room an hour after sunset. The sky above New Rio was a dark blue, the lights of the vast city starting to snap on. New Rio was a multilevel city, its buildings linked by a crosshatch of ramps. The lights illuminating the twisting, circling ramps flashed on and off, in soft pastel shades. Political slogans glowed on the sides of government buildings.

"Who was your fifth-grade Ceramic Therapy teacher?"

Thad saw Lyle Gunder, the large blond Total Security agent, rocking in a mosaic chair in a dark corner of the Walbrook Enterprises office. "Miss Cooper," he answered.

"Ah ha!" Gunder bounced out of the chair. "Caught you; it was Miss Santos."

"Only for the first part of the semester. Then Miss Santos ran off with a potter."

Gunder sank back into his tile rocker. "You're absolutely right," he admitted. "Be smug while you can. I've finally got hold of Robert B. Walbrook I's complete medical dossier, which we originally thought was lost when Detroit and environs went blooey. It's going to be fax-phoned down here to New Rio shortly. Care to submit to a few little—?"

"Hold off on the inquisition, Gunny." Lon was standing beside a long tin desk on which sat a television receiver.

"Why this twilight meeting?" Thad asked him.

"Only following my beloved gramp's wishes. He wants you to be filled in on everything, unc," smiled Lon. "Tomorrow I'll try to haul you out to our Brasilia facility. You haven't seen that yet either."

"This is all a whopping mistake on the old coot's part," Gunder grunted up out of the chair. "What was your favorite book when you were ten?"

"*The Beasts of Tarzan.*" Thad inclined his head at the TV screen. "Some kind of private view, Lon?"

Lon laughed. "You can bet your keaster on that, unc. Very private."

Gunder stalked to the door. "I'm going to watch over at the TSA building. We've got our own spy cameras watching. Don't say I didn't warn you." He left the two of them in the dim room.

Thad asked, "Is JeanAnne coming?"

"Sis claims she's still unsettled by Doc Nally's little chimp demo this afternoon," said Lon. "If you ask me, I think she's going to sneak out of her rooms at the Zombador Hotel and cruise the bars. She's got a great fondness for low-life saloons and—"

"What do you want me to see?"

"Another Hellhound test," replied Lon. "But of a different model."

"I got the impression this afternoon there was more than one version of the thing. How is this one different?"

Lon touched the side of the receiver. "Much more sophisticated, unc."

A picture blossomed on the screen. It showed a public

square, fringed with artificial palm trees, filling up with people.

"This is over in the workers' part of New Rio, near the edge," explained Lon. "Our man will be speaking at a street rally in a few minutes. Though with these Latin bastards you find a very cavalier attitude toward getting started on time." He picked up a sheet of faxpaper. "Doc Nally and I figured we'd do these guys in order, the way they are on the list."

"What list?"

Smiling, Lon dropped the paper into a drawer of the tin desk. "We have the names of a dozen men, most of whom belong to, or are suspected of belonging to, a left-wing organization they call the South American Organization of States. Two of them are here in Brazil, one in Peru . . . and so on. Gunder's buddies made up the list and our respected President Parkinson approved the final version and gave us the go-ahead on this whole field-test operation."

Thad crossed to the desk. "Wait now," he said. "I'm starting to get—"

"Right you are, unc. Walbrook Enterprises is now in the assassination business."

"Who the hell authorized that?"

"Gramps, Dad, and me," the smiling Lon told him. "You were still wandering around in the wilderness when everything was set up and okayed, unc."

"Johnny would never—"

"Sure he would. We're talking about a two- or three-billion-dollar contract here. Oops, there's Quartel. Top of

the list and considered very dangerous to the best interests of the United States in Latin America."

"I'm not going to let you—"

"Much too late to stop, unc."

No sound came out of the viewing unit. A crowd of
three hundred people was in the square now, waving and
shouting as a chunky man of fifty was lifted onto the back
of a landtruck. He greeted them with both hands held
high over his head.

"The old Hellhound should catch up with him in a very
short time," explained Lon. "One of TSA's boys is supposed to release it the minute Quartel shows."

Thad shook his head. He asked, "How do you know it
will find him? Him specifically?"

"This model is considerably more sophisticated than
the battlefield version," said Lon. "It can be set to go after
one specific person. You do that, unc, by feeding in a lot
of info, including brain-wave patterns and such like.
What it adds up to is there's only one person in the world
who matches the total picture the little Hellhound has
been fed. It won't give up till it finds that person. Once it
does and strikes, it takes off and, at a safe distance, self-
destructs."

Thad didn't say anything. He rested his fists on the desk
edge, leaning toward the small screen. Quartel had begun
to speak to the crowd.

"Eventually this particular version of the Hellhound
will bring Walbrook Enterprises a lot more revenue than
the military one," continued Lon. "Sometimes we go six
months or even a year without a significant war, but annoying politicians are always with us. You came back

from the dead at exactly the right time, unc. Walbrook
Enterprises is on the rise once . . . hey, there he goes!"

Quartel's body was quivering. He doubled, clutching
himself, silently screaming. Then he pitched off the truck
and was hidden by the crowd.

"Just like the chimps," said Lon.

CHAPTER 17

JeanAnne walked close to the edge of the rose-yellow ramp. Down below was an intricacy of walkways. In the night-black sky above the tallest tower, fireworks were erupting. Great splashes of blue, scarlet, and gold. "They aren't celebrating anything. The current President of Brazil just likes fireworks. It happens every night at this time," she said. "Why did you want to come out for a stroll, uncle?"

Beside her Thad said, "It's a little tougher for anyone to overhear us outdoors. Let's keep moving."

"Why are you afraid of being overheard, uncle?"

Thad said, "For one thing, because I'm not your uncle."

She turned her face toward his. "No, I didn't think you were."

"You didn't?"

"You're very good at it, and I know you've got Grandfather and some of the others convinced," said the girl. "But you simply are not a Walbrook. I can sense you don't have the inside coldness and ruthlessness we all carry around with us."

"Even you?"

"Me especially," said the girl. "Lon's right about me. I'm really a very mean and destructive—"

"I have a different opinion. And later on we'll go into it

in detail. Right now, JeanAnne, there's something else which—"

"There was some other kind of test tonight, wasn't there?" she asked. "I know it was something even nastier than this afternoon, because of the way Lon insisted I shouldn't miss it."

"Yeah, it's worse. They're testing it on people."

"People?" She slowed, caught hold of his arm.

"Tonight on a man named Quartel. He was—"

"Yes, I heard it on the news. They said it was some kind of stroke."

"It was a Hellhound. A variation capable of seeking out a specific person."

"Father and Lon," she said. "They . . . I don't know. I didn't really know about . . . all about this Hellhound Project, all the details, until we got down here."

"Lon has a list of another eleven men they want to use it on," said Thad. "I'm going to get that list. Then I've got to get all the information I have to the people I'm working for."

JeanAnne asked, "Who are they?"

"The Opposition Party."

The girl nodded her head up and down slowly several times. "Yes, they're not a bad bunch." She moved her hand down his arm and took hold of his hand. "Why are you confessing . . . no, that's not the exactly right word . . . why are you confiding in me?"

"Because I'm going to have to give up my Robert Walbrook I identity now and get out of Brazil fast."

JeanAnne said, "You could have done that without seeing me."

"Okay, I like you, JeanAnne," he said. "I wanted to—"

"You were somebody else before you came to us," Jean-Anne said. "Where was that? Did you leave a family behind, wife and kids and all that?"

Thad watched the night sky, the exploding flowers of color. "I was living on Manhattan when OP recruited me."

"Manhattan," she said. "In what capacity?"

"As a bum," he said, facing her. "What I was before that, with wife and reasonable job, I, one day, got tired of. It didn't seem like something I wanted to continue."

"Yes," said the girl slowly, "I know that feeling."

"So I left it all," he said. "Well, not quite that quickly. I settled my estate, took care of my effects."

"When you finish here," JeanAnne asked him, "you're not going—?"

"Not back to Manhattan, no," he said, grinning. "Not back to what I was before that either."

She exhaled, smiling. "Being around us can't have had that positive effect on you."

"The time on Manhattan, three years it was," he said, "seems to be something I went through and it's over. I guess, in part, I accepted this job so I'd have an excuse to end it. The pay is good, too."

She watched him for several quiet seconds. "Listen, how are you going to get out of New Rio and away?"

"Arrange with a local contact for transportation out."

"Don't," she said. "I'll take you back to the United States. I can borrow an aircruiser out at the family field and—"

"No, it may not be safe."

"I want to. Or don't you trust me?"

"I trust you."

"Then we'll do it," said JeanAnne. "How long is it going to take you?"

"Give me two hours."

"Fine. I won't pack, since lord knows who's watching my hotel. I'll visit a few bistros and slip away to the field. Meet me in hangar 6." She paused. "I suppose it's proper for a niece to kiss her great-uncle in public."

Dr. Nally made a fretful noise. "I can't say, my boy, that I fully approve."

"You don't have to approve, Prof." Lon was seated at a long off-white lab table. "You work for Walbrook Enterprises, which is me."

"I assumed we were going to stick to the authorized list."

"This will make it a baker's dozen," said Lon. "I've just obtained, due to considerable effort and ingenuity on Gunny's part, and without exactly his knowledge, the real medical records of my dear uncle. So now you have but to assist me in programming this little Hellhound."

"I can't possibly—"

"You will, or you'll be out on your tail, Prof. We don't need you beyond this stage."

"If I assist you, my boy," said Dr. Nally carefully, "I expect to be—"

"I'll put you on my list of especially nifty people," Lon assured him. He chuckled down inside himself. "After we get this thing ready I want you to wait about an hour before activating it."

"Surely, you don't need to worry about an alib—"

"No, no. But I want to be with dear old unc when this gadget starts looking for Robert B. Walbrook I," he said. "See, it'll solve our identity problem once and for all, a lot quicker than Gunny's methods."

"Ah," said the black scientist. "Yes, that will be interesting. Be sure to make very careful observations."

"You can bet your butt I will," Lon promised. "Now let's get to work, Prof."

CHAPTER 18

The robots let him in without any trouble. Thad stepped into an ascension tube and was carried up to the tower office.

The fireworks were still going on in the clear black sky. A huge Brazilian flag, all made of bursts of colored fire, was rippling above the towers of New Rio.

The blue, white, and green of the flag were reflected on the tin desk as Thad approached it. The list was in the drawer where Lon had dropped it that afternoon.

Thad made a copy with Lon's portable copier, which was sitting on a corner of the desk. He was folding the thin page into an inner pocket when he heard the gentle whoosh of someone rising in the tube.

There was a private exit on the other side of the room. You could only use it from inside. He sprinted to that and pushed out into the night. The narrow ramp connecting the tower to the nearest walkway was tinted a pale orange.

Up in the night a patriotic tableau was exploding.

Thad started to run.

"Hold it!" shouted Lyle Gunder.

Stopping, Thad turned toward the approaching Total Security agent. "Marisue McClean," he said.

Gunder held a stungun aimed at him. "What?"

"The name of the girl I was in love with back in the second grade," said Thad. "Just remembered."

"What were you doing up here?"

"I own the place, remember?"

Gunder said, "If you were Robert B. Walbrook I, you would. But we both know you aren't."

"Do we?"

The large blond man grunted. "We will pretty damn quick," he said as he pushed the gun to within a few inches of Thad's chest. "The medical dossier on Walbrook I, the real Walbrook, has come in. If you don't mind, I'd like you to come on over to the local TSA lab for a few simple tests."

"First thing in the morning," said Thad with a grin.

"First thing now!" Gunder prodded him with the barrel of the stungun.

Thad dropped to the ramp. He brought his head up straight into the big agent's groin.

"Yow!" The weapon leaped from Gunder's big fist.

It was light enough to break through the invisible force barrier protecting the ramp. It went spinning, sparkling as various kinds of light hit it, down and down through the interlacing of ramps.

"You son of a bitch," said Gunder, bent over.

Thad hit him twice more, fighting in the style he'd picked up during his years on Manhattan. He hit Gunder once again.

The large agent's knees jabbed into the ramp surface. He swayed, fell toward the edge. He bumped hard into the unseen guard screen and that slammed him over in the opposite direction. He fell on his left side, his body gradually spreading out into a sharp-angle sprawl.

Thad left him and ran again.

Dr. Nally yawned. He shook his head, squinting at the tiny Hellhound on the off-white table before him. Then, frowning, he glanced up from the table. He sniffed at the air in the room as he looked at the air-conditioner outlet above him.

Then he fell forward onto his work.

After some thirty seconds a figure, wearing a WE-brand gas mask, slipped into the room.

Nudging the slumped and snoring black doctor aside, the figure began to make some adjustments in the Hellhound. Using equipment, papers, and charts drawn out of a flat tan briefcase.

A few moments later the figure produced a second Hellhound missile from out of the case. That tiny missile was also worked on.

When Dr. Nally awakened fifteen minutes later, there was again only the single Hellhound on the table before him. He listened to his voxwatch. After it told him the time he said, "I'm not taking enough antisleep pills obviously. Have to up the dosage."

He picked up the miniature missile, carried it to a window, and released it.

It started to rain. A warm, slow rain. Lon ducked under the plyoawning of the cafe, poking a finger into the squat Brazilian. "What do you mean, simp?"

"Very sorry, senhor," apologized the man. "I lost her."

The rain formed glistening balls on the see-through awning. "Where? Where was she last?"

"As I told you, senhor, she vanished somehow out of the Passaro Grande Club up on level 23," explained the WE security man. "That was nearly an hour ago. I returned here to watch her hotel across the way." He had thick, spiky eyebrows, which he raised now. "Perhaps she is with your venerable uncle, Senhor Rob—"

"No, she's not. Or rather, I don't know if she is or she isn't. Your associate who was watching unc is equally good at keeping track of people, and he's lost him."

"I am truly sorry, senhor."

Lon stepped back out into the warm rain. It was over an hour since he'd left the Walbrook Enterprises labs. By now the tiny Hellhound was in flight, seeking out its target. "Damn, I want to be near unc now."

The fireworks were still going on, despite the weather. The sky above the intricacy of ramps was full of blurred bright flowers of fire.

Lon decided to go up to the Passaro Grande and ask his own questions. It was pretty certain unc and JeanAnne were together someplace. Maybe he could find out something that simp from security hadn't.

He passed a row of vendors, a stand selling lifetime flowers, a coffee cart, and one fat woman peddling bootleg sugar cane.

Lon slowed a few feet beyond the last vendor. A very odd feeling was developing in his shoulders and across the back of his head. He looked over his shoulder, frowning.

"Oh, Jesus!" he said.

He could actually see the thing coming for him. Tiny as it was, he saw it droning through the soft-falling rain.

He began to run. "That bastard Nally."

Lon had the impression he could hear the Hellhound, too.

His foot suddenly slipped on a water-slick stretch of ramp. He fell. "That bastard Nally set me up instead of—"

Scrambling upright, he ran again.

But the Hellhound was almost upon him.

Lon made a dive, trying to get off the ramp. The unseen protective screen stopped him. "Oh, Jesus, Jesus!" He tried to climb up the invisible wall.

That was where it caught him. Three feet off the ground, hands clawing at nothing.

Lon dropped to the ramp and the rain began to beat down on him.

Up in the black sky more flowers blossomed.

CHAPTER 19

The aircab stopped, hovering, four feet above the mud. "Would you mind leaping out, senhor?" the driver asked Thad. "This is as close as I like to get to all that filth."

"I'm used to it." Thad paid the fare, went down through the bottom hatch. He gripped the edge of the opening, swung back and forth a few times and let go. He landed on a length of nearwood planking which stretched between two scrapshacks.

"You don't wish me to wait, do you?"

"No, I'll get another cab out." Thad was sure he hadn't been followed down here to the poverty sector of New Rio which lay beyond the elevated part of the city. Still it was safer not to leave the cab hanging up there.

"Good luck to you, senhor." The craft zoomed upward through the rain.

The shack on Thad's left was made of the sides of old freezers, topped with a roof ripped from a war-surplus tank. Beyond it, lopsided in the muddy earth, was a hut constructed out of pseudofood cartons and the doors of junked aircabs. A one-legged man was relieving himself against its wall.

Thad walked, tightrope style, along the planking, jumping next to a warped airplane wing which served as a link between the next shacks.

Mud splashed up when he hit. A rat, water-soaked, lay dead beside the wing. Thad continued through the cluster of a thousand shacks and huts. The rain tore at him, causing him to lurch against a fence of nearwood scraps. Up ahead, across a bridge of large-size soy-can lids, stood the shack he wanted. It was made of the parts of three gutted robot jukeboxes, all strips of silver and gold paint and circles of scarlet and green light. The roof was a thatch of chrome tubing.

Thad knocked on the door just above the speaker grid.

After a moment the bright door inched open. "What do you have to say to me?"

"Otenta chavenas do cha tepido," Thad said into the dimness of the hut.

"I think that's the password."

"What else would it be?" He pushed into the scrap-shack.

The old woman who'd opened the door was holding a shining new blaster pistol. "You better say the password one more time."

"Otenta chavenas do cha tepido."

"Yes, that's it." After holstering the weapon in the wide belt wrapped round her one-piece dress, the gaunt woman crossed the floor to thump a bare foot on a batch of chrome. "What do you think of this place, by the way?"

"A little flamboyant maybe."

"It suits me." She lifted the chunk of flooring, fetched out a pixphone. "The only thing I don't like is the rats.

They ate my last phone, or at least they carried it off to their lair. Or nest. What do you call a rat's—?"

"Could you wait outside while I make the call?"

"You can talk in front of me. I've got a top clearance with OP."

Picking up the special phone, Thad punched out the number Crosby Rich had given him. In a moment the stocky man's face appeared on the small rectangle of screen. "I've got something for you," Thad told him.

The old woman was squatting in a corner, hunting cockroaches with her thumb.

"Good, because a dumbbell thing has happened here and I'm not sure what it means."

"What?"

"Give me what you've got first."

Thad told Rich what he'd found out about the Hellhound.

The Opposition Party troubleshooter said, "Little teenie-weenie missiles, huh? That's a bitch of an idea."

The old woman cleared her throat.

"They've already used it once down here," continued Thad. "If you've heard about the death of a guy named Quartel up there yet, it was the Hellhound that did it. And they've picked eleven more targets." He took out the list he'd swiped, read the names to Rich. "You've got to make all this public. That should discourage them until the whole operation can be closed down."

"Isn't there . . . didn't you say there was some defense against the Hellhound?"

"Yeah, but I don't have it. They've got that stuff stored out at the WE labs."

Rich had picked up a kelp brioche and was about to take a bite. "Hey, it occurs to me," he said, lowering the roll. "Maybe this dumbbell thing that's happened here ties in."

"You haven't told me."

"Dr. Rosenfeld has disappeared, been gone nearly a day," said Rich. "When we checked out his offices we found someone had snatched—"

"My medical records?" asked Thad, his hand tightening on the pixphone receiver.

"Exactly. Do you—?"

"Holy Christ! They're going to send one of those Hellhounds after me."

"I thought you said you drank some repellent?"

"That oral stuff only protects for an hour or two."

"Well, they could simply be—"

Thad hung up, spun, and ran for the door.

"Bad news?" asked the old woman as he plunged out into the rain and mud.

The doors of the pillbar snapped open and a fat man in a wrinkled tourist suit came tottering out. He stumbled, one knee jabbing down into a water-filled pothole. His suit pockets rattled, a beer-bottle-brown container of capsules hopped out to go bouncing then rolling along the rainy street.

Thad had reached the end of the poverty belt and was in the strip of specialty saloons which rimmed the elevated core of New Rio. He hit again the summoning button on the aircab box screwed to the noryl front of the bar. It was now eleven minutes since he'd talked to Crosby Rich.

"Come here; come here," the fat man told the rolling pill bottle.

Thad turned, hurried over to the man. "Let me help you." He retrieved the container, placed it in the fat palm. "Can I help you to your vehicle?"

"That would certainly be a gracious gesture, sir," said the fat tourist as he straightened up. "I can tell by your appearance you are not a footpad nor a—"

"Where is it?"

"Where is it?" While he thought, the fat man absently uncapped the pill cylinder and shook two orange-and-black capsules into his hand. "This is a prewar antibiotic. Can't get it in the states. Makes me feel good all over and—"

"Is it a landcar or an aircruiser?"

"One of those, yes," replied the dazed pill freak. "Here's the tag for it, right here." He reached into his coat pocket, causing tiny bottles and boxes to come cascading out to fall to the wet street.

Thirteen minutes gone now. Thad scanned the night around him. He saw only heavy raindrops. No sign of a minute Hellhound missile. He thrust his own hand into the fat man's pocket. He located the round plastic parking tag. "Wait right here; I'll bring it."

On his hands and knees the fat man was gathering up his scattered pills. "I'll take a handful of these blue ones while I'm waiting your return, sir. Very good for chills and fevers, in case I come down with . . ."

The man was renting a black-and-silver aircruiser. It was decked on the top level of a five-level, automatic

parking tower around the corner from the bar. The tag
admitted Thad to the upper floor.

He climbed in, started the cruiser, and flew away into
the dark. Fifteen minutes had gone by.

The cyborg watchman scratched at the platinum side of
his head with three silver fingers and two of flesh. "This is
sort of embarrassing, Senhor Walbrook," he said. He was
standing in the doorway of the main WE lab building,
looking out at Thad.

The night rain was falling heavy, rattling down through
the branches and leaves of the decorative gardens. "It's
important I get in," Thad said. Twenty-two minutes.

"I realize that, and I know you are now one of the head
men in all of Walbrook Enterprises," said the cyborg.
"The thing is, senhor, I've no authorization to admit you.
I'm certain it's simply negligence on someone's part, but
I—"

Thad swung out and hit the man twice on the jaw. He'd
selected a spot which was flesh and bone.

The watchman sighed. His real eye and his noryl-plastic eye clicked shut simultaneously as he collapsed to the
floor.

Thad took the man's keys and admittance tags away
from him before he'd settled into his final slumped posi-
tion.

The room containing the anti-Hellhound materials was
at the far end of the building as Thad recalled.

He was nearly there when a door slid open. Dr. E. Jack
Nally stepped out into the corridor, yawning.

"Oops," he said when he saw Thad. "Now, Mr. Walbrook, let me assure you I had nothing to do—"

Thad pushed him aside. The anti-Hellhound room was three doors farther on. Twenty-nine minutes.

"Good heavens!" exclaimed Dr. Nally behind him. "There it comes."

Thad broke into a run, looking back over his shoulder. A tiny flash of copper seemed to be floating down the dim corridor, patiently, toward him.

He hit the door, dived into the room. The heavy door should stop it. What had Nally said about how the damn things worked indoors? Would it wait outside for him, or get in here somehow?

He sprinted to the wall cabinet where the spray-on anti-Hellhound repellent was kept, jerked open the door. The cabinet was empty.

Thad took a quick deep breath, then began to search the room.

"Here we go," he said aloud.

The container was resting on a small table in the corner. He caught it up, sprayed repellent over himself, liberally. Next he located, in another cabinet, the locket-type device Nally had shown them in the afternoon. Thad hung it round his neck, flicked it on.

A faint pinging sounded above him. Thad looked up to see something emerge from the air-conditioning outlet. It was the Hellhound.

It came diving straight down at him.

Two feet short of his face it halted, fluttering. It dropped suddenly to the floor.

Thad, absently stroking the talisman round his neck, stepped round the Hellhound. He went out into the hall.

Dr. Nally was still there. "How does this affect my future with Walbrook Enterprises?" he asked.

CHAPTER 20

The robot's mouth dropped open, its wire eyebrows rose an inch, and its vinyl eyes rolled. "What a surprise to see you, senhor."

"What?" Thad said to the grease-monkey robot.

They were standing in the rain in front of hangar 6 on the Walbrook Enterprises private field. The hangar glowed with soft orange light and it was yawningly empty.

A tiny squeegee came extending out of the robot's fingertip so that it could wipe the raindrops from its metal face. "Care to have me squeegee you off, senhor?"

"No," said Thad. "Has Miss Walbrook been here?"

"*Sim,*" replied the mechanical grease monkey as its squeegee retracted. "Plus also Senhor Walbrook."

"Which Walbrook? Lon?"

"Not Senhor Lon, no. The gentleman with the *gago* . . . the stutter."

Thad took a few steps toward the empty hangar. "Alex?" Alex was supposed to be home in Connecticut.

"That is who it was, senhor," replied the robot, trailing after him. "He is, you will pardon me for saying it, not a very memorable gentleman. If it were not for the stam—"

"Miss Walbrook went with him?"

The grease monkey's metal head made a slight creak as he nodded affirmatively. "*Sim,* yes." He rubbed at his neck. "Excuse the unseemly sounds. I always seem to get raspy-sounding in this damp weather. The next time you're in the WE robotics plant in Rotterdam you might mention—"

"They took off in an aircruiser?"

"*Sim,*" answered the robot. "In the very ship Senhorina Walbrook had me warm up for her."

Thad walked on into the hangar, glancing absently around. "Why would she take off with Alex? Where were they supposed to be going?"

"Why, to your bedside I imagine, senhor."

Thad's left eye narrowed. "Alex told her I was sick?"

"Injured, in an aircab accident," said the grease monkey. "If I may say so, senhor, the young lady must be quite fond of you. She grew pale as *neve* . . . that is, snow . . . when she heard you were injured. You certainly must have remarkable recuperative powers, I—"

"Where was I supposed to have had this accident?"

"Ah, that is an interesting point, senhor. The gentleman . . . Alex you said his name is? . . . he told the young lady you'd had the accident in New Rio. Yet they didn't head in that direction."

Thad said, "I wonder where the hell he took her."

"We can ask Borboleta."

"Who's he?"

"The flight-tower computer. He keeps track of all our ships. That's his nickname, Borboleta. It means . . . what is it in your tongue? . . . yes, butterfly. Borboleta, he's a little bit"—the grease monkey's hand fluttered in the air —"swish, as you say. But a very efficient computer otherwise."

They went out into the rain to ask the computer where Alex and JeanAnne were heading.

It told them.

CHAPTER 21

Down below in the black, blurry night, giant strips of light spelled out BRASILIA/100 Miles. Near that was another, which read See Authentic Headhunter Village! Adults—$25, Kids—$10. All this was repeated, in smaller strips of light, in Portuguese.

Thad readjusted the course dial of the control panel of the aircruiser he'd borrowed back at the WE field. Toward the small view screen set in the dash's center he said, "Is there someone there with you?"

Crosby Rich shook his head impatiently. "No, it's our dumbbell President. He's taken over everybody's television set for another speech."

Off, out of eye range, Warren Parkinson was saying, "My press secretary was going to read this important message to you, my fellow Americans, but then he came down with a virus. I, and I hope the press won't make much ado about this, don't like to have people with colds and sniffles around me. Not that I'm in bad health or anything. You remember I told you all the other day . . ."

By talking loudly Rich faded the President of the United States out. "Do you have any idea what's going on?" he asked Thad.

"Alex Walbrook is making some kind of play," he said. "It seems to include his taking JeanAnne with him out to

Brasilia. Walbrook Enterprises has some kind of facility out there."

"Artifacts."

"Huh?"

"WE manufactures imitation Americana artifacts at their Brasilia plant," Rich explained. "Brasilia's the biggest flea market in the Americas and that's probably why WE is there. Listen, Thad . . . you don't think maybe the girl is being used as a decoy, to get you out there?"

"No," said Thad. "I'm fairly sure Alex thinks I'm dead."

"Oh, that's right"—Rich remembered—"somebody was going to put a Hellhound on your trail. Did they?"

"Yeah, but I got hold of the repellents in time," Thad said. "Dr. Nally admitted Lon was the one who sent the thing after me, but I figure Alex must have—"

"Can't be Lon," cut in Rich. "Unless he used one of those dumbbell things to kill himself."

"He's dead?"

"Just got the report on it," said Rich. "They found him on a pedestrian ramp dead. Official release by the New Rio police's public relations department lists the cause of Lon's death as a stroke. From what you've told us, though, I'd guess the Hellhound got him."

"Have you made the list of targets public?"

"What do you think Parkinson is on the air for. He's denying everything, but I don't think they'll be able to use any of the Hellhounds now," said Rich. "We're sending a bunch of OP field men to New Rio to try to clean things up on that end."

"You'll find Dr. Nally in a closet at the lab," said Thad.

"I've got all the repellent and the model Hellhounds with me."

"Good," said Rich. "You really think Alex is behind the attempts on you and Lon?"

"It would sure explain why he's down here," answered Thad. "Why he's grabbed JeanAnne. I'm afraid he's maybe planning some kind of accident for her. If Alex didn't believe I was dead, he wouldn't have openly stepped in. It doesn't fit with the character he's been hiding behind. To think me dead, he has to be in on sending a Hellhound after me and—"

"The other accidents."

"Would I," President Parkinson was saying, "use an engine of destruction, even a tiny little one such as these alleged Hellhounds, on our political foes? I tell you certainly not, not when we already have in the arsenal of the United States the weapons of truth, of . . ."

Thad said, "It could be Alex was behind those attempts to kill me at the Connecticut estate."

"What's his reason?"

"Maybe he's not happy with his progress upward in WE."

"I can rush a couple crack OP agents to you in Brasilia," offered the stocky troubleshooter. "To help you force your way into the WE plant."

"I'm not going to force my way in," Thad told him. "I'm going to walk in like I own the place."

The Walbrook Enterprises hangars in Brasilia were tinted see-through domes. As Thad eased his cruiser into hangar *otto,* he spotted a ship in the next hangar which fit the description of the one Alex and JeanAnne had taken off from New Rio in.

Climbing out of his ship, he asked the hangar attendant, "Did that aircruiser over there come in tonight?"

"Could I interest you in a wrist watch, senhor?" The small man had several strapped to his left arm, from wrist to elbow. "Old-fashioned, nonspeaking kind. Not your shoddy contemporary imitations but authenticated timepieces from the 20th century. They all work perfectly; you can hear them ticking." He offered his arm to Thad.

"The cruiser," Thad repeated.

"*Sim,* it arrived . . . oh, maybe two hours ago," replied the ticking attendant.

"Who was in it?"

"I also have some nice pocket watches. These, I swear to you on my mother's honor, are actually from the late 19th century."

"Who landed?"

"Another Senhor Walbrook," answered the small man as he fished round golden watches out of the various pockets on the front of his coverall. "His name, I think, is Alex Walbrook, and there was with him a young lady, Miss Walbrook."

"Where'd they go?"

"She did not seem in the best of condition," said the attendant. "Very drowsy, wobbly when she walked. I suppose, as you could well testify, the pressures at the top level are—"

"Did they head for the Walbrook Enterprises plant?"

"I believe so, Senhor Walbrook."

"How far is that from here?"

"It is but a few short blocks. Once you leave the field, walk straight down Avenue Liberdade. You cannot miss the gigantic W and E on the face of the building," the small man explained. "You're sure to enjoy the walk, since the rain has diminished to practically nothing, and this route will take you through the most interesting vending section in all the Brasilia flea market. If you'd like a larger clock, say a grandfather, see my cousin who—"

Thad was already out of the hangar, striding for the gate.

On Liberdade the rain drifted gently down, a misty drizzle.

The dealer nearest the gate, sheltered by a cluster of plyumbrellas, was hawking authentic 20th-century appliances. "You no doubt would like to possess a real 1970 Kenmore 2-speed, 3-cycle washer, senhor," he called to Thad.

Thad kept moving.

He passed vendors of three-piece suits from 1980, see-through suits from 1990, feathers and pseudofeathers from several eras, sellers of antique beer cans, soft-drink bottles, and real tobacco cigarettes, an entire square devoted to the selling of automobile, landcar, and aircruiser parts. All of it crowded in among the fragile-seeming towers and ramps of the city.

Then up ahead on his left he noticed the WE monogram glowing ten stories up on the side of a thin spire of a building.

From beside a vending cart filled with musical flowers, a big blocky man stepped. "Hey, old buddy, I want to talk to you," he called at Thad, "real bad."

It was Lyle Gunder.

CHAPTER 22

The floor was a clear pale yellow, one-way, see-through material. It gave a view of one of the large workshops down below the office suite. The night-shift robots, watched over by a lone human foreman, were assembling imitation 20th-century washers and stoves. The foreman, a dry, tan old man, couldn't see who was above him, but he seemed to sense someone was. His glance continually flicked upward.

JeanAnne watched the four-armed robots fitting the white parts together for a few moments longer. Then, shaking her head, she pushed herself up from the floating cot she'd found herself lying on. After taking a breath in, she asked, "This the Brasilia plant?"

"Yes . . . uh . . . that's where we are." Alex was sitting on the edge of a rose-filled chair.

"I take it," said the girl as she swung her slim legs over the edge of the cot, "Uncle Robert didn't really have an accident."

"The little . . . uh . . . story I spun for you back in New Rio was . . . uh . . . not true."

"What are you really doing in Brazil?"

"Looking after my own interests," he replied, smiling his inadequate smile. "As I mentioned earlier your . . . uh . . . father and . . . uh . . . old JP believe I am merely delivering some relatively unimportant messages to various . . . uh . . . Latin American subsidiaries."

Down in the workshop the foreman was arguing with a robot.

JeanAnne said, "If Uncle Robert didn't have an accident . . . how did you know I was going to be at that hangar?"

"Oh, I . . . uh . . . I'm very good at finding out things. It's one of the advantages of being visually uninteresting."

"Why'd you give me that knockout shot? Why'd you bring me here?"

Alex's smile faded away. "I'm afraid you're going to have an . . . uh . . . accident."

She said, "An accident?" She watched him for a long silent moment. "You're the one then? The one who tried to kill us with that damn gamekeeper robot."

"I'm . . . uh . . . very good with things mechanical," he answered. "Though your dear father has never bothered to notice that. Yes, I adjusted the robot so it would kill you. I tinkered with the snowboat as well."

"Neither one worked quite right," said the girl. "Which is typical of you, Uncle Alex."

"Your forthcoming . . . uh . . . accident will succeed," he promised. "Just as Lon's has."

"Lon?" She stood up and away from the cot, her feet slightly unsteady. "What have you done to Lon?"

"I . . . uh . . . did nothing directly," said Alex. "It's the Hellhound I was able to fool with, and modify, which did it."

"You sent a Hellhound after him?"

"That's where the . . . uh . . . humor comes in. You

see, Lon was intending to try the little missile out on Robert I," he told her. "We're a wonderful family, aren't we?" Another laugh rattled out of him. "What's so . . . uh . . . splendid about this is that none of them can openly admit what . . . uh . . . actually happened to poor Lon. The Hellhound Project must be kept . . . uh . . . absolutely secret, no matter what. And they'll never suspect . . . uh . . . clumsy Alex of having a hand in any of this. Oh, it's . . . uh . . . beautiful."

JeanAnne clasped her hands tightly together. "Why are —?" She didn't complete the sentence.

"Yes?" Alex spread his feet wide on the view floor so he could better observe the workshop below.

"I was going to ask you why you're doing this, but I guess I know."

"Yes, I simply want to . . . uh . . . control the whole thing," answered her uncle. "All these years that's . . . uh . . . been my notion as I went about patiently arranging things."

"All the other accidents in the family, the deaths, were your—?"

"There were no accidents," smiled Alex. "As I say, I've been patient. The return of Robert I, however, has forced me to act again a bit . . . uh . . . sooner than I intended."

"I thought you were glad to have your father back."

"My father's dead," said Alex. "Once, a long time ago, I would have . . . uh . . . been happy over his returning. But he left me there too long, too long alone with all the rest of them."

"But he is alive."

"No, Robert Walbrook I is dead. He's been dead, really

dead and not pseudodead, for eight years. When the plague hit Detroit, I . . . uh . . . saw an opportunity to place myself one step closer to complete control of Walbrook Enterprises. I sent . . . uh . . . immunized agents into that chaos where the plague and riots raged. They made absolutely certain no bodies remained in the storage vault."

"You could order your own father—?"

"He could leave me alone with them," answered Alex. "Yes, I can do whatever I have to do. I know what . . . uh . . . most of you think of me. But now . . . uh . . . very soon it won't matter. Not any longer. I was going to wait a bit, but there was a danger of this impostor being unmasked by Gunder or someone else. Then the . . . uh . . . real fate of my late father might have come to light."

"I'm in your way, too?"

"I'm sure this . . . uh . . . imitation Robert I confided in you, JeanAnne," her uncle said. "Once you are gone, it will leave only a feeble old man and your father between me and—"

"What about Uncle Robert? Real or otherwise, he's still one of the heads of Walbrook Enterprises."

"Oh, he's safely . . . uh . . . dead by now," replied Alex. "I sent a second Hellhound after him hours ago, using his actual medical records to feed it."

The girl dropped to the floating cot. "You killed him, too? Just like—"

"Yes, just like Lon and Quartel and those poor . . . uh . . . sad chimpanzees." Alex rose up. "Now, it really is time to do something about you, JeanAnne."

CHAPTER 23

"They're not supposed to use it on each other," Gunder, the Total Security agent, said. A large bunch of daisies on the vending cart began playing a loud military march. Gunder grabbed up the trick flowers and tossed them off into the drizzly night.

"What the hell, senhor?" complained the aged vendor.

"Here's fifty bucks. Keep all that crap quiet."

The vendor took the bills and began, cautiously, pushing his cart away from the two men.

"You're talking about," Thad asked the agent, "the Hellhound?"

"I'm talking about the Hellhound, the President of the United States is talking about the Hellhound," growled Gunder, "the entire damn news media of the world is talking about the Hellhound. All on account of you, chum."

"Is that why you're here, Gunder, to get revenge?"

"It's too late for that now," said Gunder. "I'm not like President Parkinson; I don't keep a shit list. Once things hit the fan, I go on to something else. And right now I'm trying to find out what all the Goddamn Walbrooks are up to."

"What did you mean about their using it on each other?" asked Thad. "Do you know for sure Alex was behind what happened to Lon?"

The TSA agent made a surprised intake of air. "How'd you come to that conclusion?"

"Well, who else would it be? Lon's dead, old JP and Bob ※2 are still up in Connecticut."

Nodding, Gunder said, "That's why I'm here in Brasilia. I been trailing Alex ever since I learned he was down here. Do you think maybe he's gone goofy?"

"Nope, he's probably only trying to put himself in control of Walbrook Enterprises," Thad said. "My return from the dead may have goosed him into accelerating his plans."

"Come on, bozo. You're not still claiming to be the original Robert?"

"No, but whoever I am, it gave Alex something unexpected to cope with."

"I finally got hold of your real medical records, you know. You're Thad McIntosh, working as a spy for the Opposition Party."

"Yeah, I know that already," said Thad, grinning. "So did Alex apparently. Since he also sent a Hellhound missile after me."

"No kidding?" Gunder slammed his fist into his palm. "I had a hunch somebody'd been diddling around with my secret files. Alex, huh? You wouldn't think a clutchbutt like him could—"

"Look," cut in Thad, "are you going to try to tangle with me now? If so, let's get to it. I want to get JeanAnne out of that plant over there before Alex—"

"You think that's why he brought her along? But she isn't in the way of his inheriting the company."

"He may think she's in the way for some other reason."

Thad stepped off the curb, crossing the street, working his way through carts and stands.

"Hey, wait up, bozo," called Gunder. "What say we collaborate?"

"Oh, so?"

"I've worked with worse bastards than OP agents," said the blocky Total Security agent. "Right now my prime objective is to stop Alex from knocking off anybody else and from using any more of those Hellhounds."

"Okay." Thad kept moving toward the WE spire.

"How you figuring on busting in?"

"I'm going to walk through the main entrance," said Thad. "Except for you and Alex, everybody human and mechanical in the Walbrook Enterprises setup thinks I'm Robert Walbrook I."

Following Thad up the curving mosaic steps of the plant building, Gunder said, "How come that didn't work for you back at the labs in New Rio? According to my sources you had to coldcock a guard to get in."

"Flying down here," said Thad, "I put in a couple of calls to WE's central security office and the Latin American office. I'm cleared for all the WE facilities now."

"That's not going to last for long," Gunder said. "They're going to figure out, the old man or somebody, you're the one who gave the Hellhound story out. If I hadn't been so damn busy with these other matters, I'd of told them myself."

"But right now we still should be able to get in," said Thad as he reached out to push the revolving entry door.

They were.

Once inside the vast two-story-high lobby, Gunder said,

"I know this building's layout. Come on with me over to the security office."

"Won't Alex have JeanAnne up in one of the executive rooms?"

"He might, but he also might have her just about any place." Gunder thrust his fingers into a print lock on a wide noryl door. "They know my hands all over the world."

After a five-second interval the door slid aside.

"Hi there, Gunny," said a tinny voice inside the blue room they entered.

A compact computer was seated on a wide floating sofa. "Hello, Chex," Gunder said to the mechanism.

"What can I do you for, Gunny?" chuckled the computer.

"It's your job to know where everybody is, Chex."

"Bet your bottom dollar."

"Okay, we want to find Alex Walbrook. Whereabouts in the plant is he?"

"That's an easy one," answered the jovial computer. "Just take a gander at monitor ⌗12 up there."

Thad and Gunder turned toward the wall which was covered with monitor screens. Number 12 was just lighting up.

"There he is in his office," said Chex.

Gunder frowned up at the television shot of an empty room. "Where?"

Chex rattled. "That's funny," it said. "Where the dickens did he get to?"

CHAPTER 24

JeanAnne tried one more scream before giving up.

Alex gestured with the blaster pistol in his hand. "As I . . . uh . . . told you," he said, "no one is going to hear you in this . . . uh . . . part of the building. Now let us continue."

They were in a narrow, down-slanting corridor behind the executive offices. The air was chill, the light a thin daylight color glowing down from the ceiling.

The dark-haired girl resumed walking.

"We'll use the short cut through the . . . uh . . . communications wing," Alex told her.

She opened the door marked *Com.*

The only illumination in the wide room came from a strip of night light over the opposite door and from the single news screen that was still going.

When the two of them were about in the middle of the room the news screen said, "Now for all our viewers with a command of the American language, here is the news in American. The big story at the moment is, without doubt, that of the Hellhound . . ."

"Uh . . . what?"

JeanAnne smiled in the shadows. "Maybe he isn't dead," she said softly to herself.

Alex poked his pistol barrel into his niece's side. "Stop here for a minute. I want to . . . uh . . . hear this."

The Brazilian newscaster had a substantial mustache, which he twisted as he spoke. "The White House press secretary is in seclusion at a cruiser lodge in New Hampshire and, other than appearing briefly to hang a Do Not Disturb sign on his doorknob, has had nothing to do with the news media. The President of the United States, however, has been quite voluble about the alleged miniature missiles which Walbrook Enterprises supposedly built under highly secret government contract. Here is some footage of President Parkinson, made only a few moments ago in Washington, D.C."

"How did the word get out?" asked Alex as he stared at the small screen.

"Uncle Robert," said the girl. "You didn't succeed in stopping him."

"I certainly didn't stop him in . . . uh . . . time, if he's the source."

"And outside of a little headache right through here and over here," President Parkinson was saying, "I feel tiptop. Allow me to take up a little more of your time, fellow Americans, and repeat what I told you earlier about these so-called Hellhounds. I know you'd probably rather be watching your favorite dramatic and game shows, but this is sort of important. Because when somebody makes fun of the President, why then he's making fun of the country and, therefore, of you and you and . . ."

"You might as well quit," JeanAnne advised Alex. "Everything's out in the open; everyone knows about the Hellhounds."

"Quiet."

"Let me say once again that I, as your President, would never authorize the construction of such a weapon as this Hellhound is said to be. Perhaps our many enemies throughout the world would fool around with something like that, but . . ."

"Fool," said Alex at the screen. "Well, let's continue, JeanAnne." He prodded her with the blaster.

"Why go ahead and do something to me, Uncle Alex? The whole Walbrook business is likely to come tumbling down now."

"Uh . . . nonsense," he told her. "The most this will do is topple old JP and, probably, your father. Then I step in and reorganize. It's . . . uh . . . perfect."

"Somebody will know you're as involved with the Hellhound missiles as they are."

"Who? Anyone who knows is dead, except you."

"Uncle Robert isn't dead. He has to be alive. He got the facts out to the Opposition Party."

"Before the Hellhound got him perhaps." He nudged the pistol barrel harder into her side. "Now hurry on through that door yonder."

Beyond the door was another down-slanting corridor. The door at its end was marked Children's Artifacts 2/Caution!

That door opened on to a catwalk over a machine-filled workshop. All robots here, no human overseer.

"What are they making?" asked the girl.

"Dolls. Right now it's something from the 20th century

known as a Raggedy Ann doll. There's a nice market for them at the moment, especially in Asia. Move on out farther on the catwalk."

"I can see fine from here."

"But you can't . . . uh . . . fall."

The girl looked into her uncle's thin face. "That's going to be my accident, is it? A fall."

"The autopsy will show you'd been drinking considerably . . . uh . . . JeanAnne," Alex said. "No one will doubt it was an accident."

She watched the unclothed dolls far below having I Love You stamped on their pink chests. She took a few steps out. "Okay, you're going to have to come out here and do it, Uncle Alex."

"Oh . . . uh . . . I intend to," he smiled, following her. "Don't think familial—" He suddenly stiffened. His right arm flapped up and down. The pistol dropped away, falling straight down into one of the doll-stuffing mechanisms.

Excelsior began spewing up in a ten-foot column. A grinding unhappy sound came from the machine. An alarm system began to make a loud pocking sound.

"Okay, Alex, let's get back inside," Thad suggested. He had one arm locked around the lean man's neck, his other hand was gripping Alex's gun arm.

"Why didn't the Hellhound kill you?"

"I outran it." Thad pulled Alex backward, got him into the corridor.

"I'll take him," offered Gunder. "See after the girl."

"No," protested Alex. "I don't want him handling me."

Thad left him with Gunder and went back out onto the catwalk.

CHAPTER 25

JeanAnne awakened and looked out the window of the aircruiser. "Afternoon," she decided after studying the sky. "Where are we roughly?"

"Two hundred miles from home," answered Thad from the piloting seat.

"You mean Connecticut or what?"

"From the U.S. border."

"Because I don't think I'm going to be making my home at the Walbrook spread anymore."

"I figured not."

"Anymore news come through while I was asleep?"

"Parkinson has issued a few more denials and mentioned he thinks he's coming down with stomach flu."

"About Alex or any of the rest of the family?"

"JP is promising a statement shortly. Gunder did go ahead and turn Alex over to the Brazilian national police," answered Thad. "They're going to see if they can prove he killed Lon."

"Lon," said the girl, hugging herself. "Did you know who that Hellhound that killed him was actually intended for?"

"Me, probably."

"Yes, exactly. From what Uncle Alex told me Lon decided it would be fun to try one out on you," JeanAnne said. "Except he seems to have believed you were really Uncle Robert and so he gave the missile the wrong medical information to work with."

"Apparently only you and Alex didn't believe in me."

"Alex had a good reason. He'd had the real Uncle Robert killed back during the Detroit troubles."

"So he knew I was a fake right from the start."

JeanAnne said, "We're a marvelous family, aren't we?"

"Some of the individual members are okay."

"What are you going to do next?"

"Report in to the Opposition Party guy who hired me, give him all the rest of what I've learned down here."

"That'll mean more busy days for Walbrook Enterprises and the Parkinson administration," the girl said. "Then what?"

"Then what for me, you mean?"

"Yes."

"I'm not sure," he answered. "Don't worry. I won't be going back to Manhattan. I think I'll see what other jobs the OP has to offer."

She smiled. "Good," she said. "By the way, what's your real name?"

"Thad McIntosh."

"Not a bad name," the girl decided. "And can you get your own face back now?"

"So they told me."

"I'd like to see that."

"You will," he promised.

"This doesn't taste much like a banana," said Crosby Rich, further unwrapping the dark brown object in his hand. "It claims to be a Nearly Authentic Imitation Dried

Banana, but it's obvious the dumbbell company never tasted a real imitation dried banana in their lives. Are you satisfied?"

Thad was standing in front of a mirror wall in a small white room inside a hidden OP facility in New Jersey. He was studying his face. "Yeah, it's about what I remember my original face being like."

"So your chances for ruling the vast Walbrook empire have faded away to nothing." Rich took another bite of the imitation banana, making a slow half circle behind Thad. "Still want to continue to work for us?"

"First I have to go to Spain." Thad turned to face him.

"Spain? Oh, that's right. The girl went over there."

"While I was here being processed back to myself."

"Turns out you were right about her. She had nothing to do with trying to kill you, or with the Hellhound business. Here that dumbbell Alex was behind all those killings and nobody tumbled."

"He's still down in Brazil?"

"Yeah, but I don't think they'll ever be able to make a case against him," answered the troubleshooter. "Several people are getting charges ready against him around here, in case he comes back home."

"Is there anybody left in the government to do anything?"

"Most of Parkinson's cabinet is hiding here and there. The President himself is holed up in the summer White House in Topeka," said Rich. "But the Senate and the House are in pretty good shape, for them."

"They going to try to impeach Parkinson?"

"Rumor is he's going to resign and have himself committed to an orthomolecular sanitarium near Topeka. Meaning the Vice-President will take over, if they can find out where he's hiding."

"Have they rounded up all the Hellhounds?"

"My boys got most of the stuff right after you left Brazil. We also got Dr. Nally, but we're going to turn him over to the TSA when the Hellhound hearings get rolling next week."

"You're co-operating with TSA?"

"During this emergency only. Same way you co-operated with that dumbbell Gunder." Rich finished up the banana. "Hey, and we found Dr. Rosenfeld. Some of Gunder's boys had grabbed him, stored him in a motel in New Hampshire, and used a truth machine on him. That's how they got your real medical records."

"Did you," asked Thad, "open that bank account for me?"

Rich said, "We opened it, but listen . . . there's only a quarter of a million in it, not a half. I'll tell you why. Eventually OP's going to pay you all we promised for the successful completion of the job. The thing is, Thad, those dumbbells in Budget—"

"A quarter of a million is fine," Thad told him. "I just wanted to be sure I have enough to get to Spain."

' Wiping his palm on his trousers, Rich held out his hand. "I'll contact you as soon as you get back, Thad," he said. "With a new job for you. How long you figure to be gone?"

Thad grinned, shrugged, and walked out of the room.